"I'm not Scrooge."

"I think you've been Scrooge for so long, you don't see it anymore.... Do you know how a Giving Tree works?"

Jonah shook his head. "Now, why would Scrooge bother to learn about something that sounds so intrinsically unprofitable?"

"Very funny, Ebenezer," Carly said. "Did anyone ever tell you that you think too much about money? You can't fool me." She touched his chest. "I know you've got a heart in here. I learned that the night...uh..." Her cheeks flamed, but she didn't move quickly enough.

Jonah covered her hand with his. "Okay, it's a bet. If I enjoy this Christmas as much as you say, you win, and I'll bring toys for every kid who wants one. If I don't, you lose. And I get..."

Carly tugged her hand free. "I know what you get."

Catherine Leigh lives in a tiny Montana town, surrounded by beautiful mountains and friendly people. The daughter of an American navy admiral, she spent the first twenty-five years of her life traveling the world, but—like her heroines—she fell in love with the Western way of life. Enthusiastically encouraged by her husband and three children, Catherine is now fulfilling her lifelong dream of becoming a writer.

Catherine loves to hear from her readers. You can write to her at:
P.O. Box 774
Ennis
MT 59729

Books by Catherine Leigh

HARLEQUIN ROMANCE®
3075—PLACE FOR THE HEART
3426—SOMETHING OLD, SOMETHING NEW
3469—REBEL WITHOUT A BRIDE

One Night Before
Christmas
Catherine Leigh

TORONTO • NEW YORK • LONDON
AMSTERDAM • PARIS • SYDNEY • HAMBURG
STOCKHOLM • ATHENS • TOKYO • MILAN • MADRID
PRAGUE • WARSAW • BUDAPEST • AUCKLAND

For my sister of the heart,
Karen Watson McMullin

ISBN 0-373-03533-0

ONE NIGHT BEFORE CHRISTMAS

First North American Publication 1998.

CHAPTER ONE

BY THE time Carly Underbrook arrived at the Gallatin Gateway Inn that evening, she didn't feel much like going to the party. The bed in the room she'd rented upstairs, and the blue flannel nightie in her overnight case, looked far more inviting.

She massaged the tightness at her temples, but she didn't have a real headache. A hot shower would soothe any tension she felt. What troubled her was her reaction to the conversation she'd had with her mother before she left.

It wasn't as though she and DeeDee hadn't had this same conversation before, the one about how many dates Carly had turned down the last five years. Of course she hadn't turned down many recently, none in fact. Within a few months of moving to Wide Spot, Montana, she'd made her position clear to the men there, and now no one asked.

Except DeeDee continued to ask—in the kindest way possible—why Carly was bent on throwing her own life away just because her father had died. But, as Carly had explained more than once, she hadn't given up living. Her life was full and satisfying. She had simply resolved never again to rely on anyone but herself.

She sighed gustily. Her talk with DeeDee tonight hadn't been all that different from many others. But something—Carly couldn't say what—had struck her differently. All the way from Wide Spot to Bozeman, a seventy-five-mile drive, she had dwelled on how solitary her existence had become the last five years.

Usually Carly kept such thoughts at bay. She thought not of how much she'd loved her father but of the mountain of debt he'd saddled her and her mother with when he died. She thought not of being lonely but of how good it felt to take care of herself.

She stood and began tugging off clothes, determined to control her thoughts tonight, as well. She turned the shower on hot, assuring herself that if she'd *really* wanted a date for this party, she'd have found one.

She hadn't come purely for her entertainment anyway. Christmas was just over a month away, and many of the arms Carly needed to twist between now and then would be downstairs at this party. Besides, she might finally get a chance to meet Jonah St. John.

The woman at the United Way office had assured Carly that this was the only Christmas party attended by Mr. St. John and his…she'd stumbled a little over what to call the woman he lived with, finally settling on Significant Other. Apparently Mr. St. John believed that the invitations he received at Christmas came only from people interested in getting donations from his wildly successful toy business.

Even in the shower, Carly blushed again at that, because it was *exactly* why she wanted to meet Jonah St. John. In fact, hers was one of the invitations he ignored every year.

Party sounds grew louder as Carly dressed and put on makeup. The freezing night outside seemed to seep into the room, and she was sorry to take off her sweater to go downstairs. By the time she reached the high-ceilinged dining room, she was shivering in her green silk dress. She rubbed her bare arms and, trying to warm up, grabbed a hot eggnog from the tray of a passing waiter. It didn't heat her all the way to the inside, but at least she quit shivering.

Carly wandered through the crowd, chatting with friends and renewing acquaintances. The combined Bozeman charities put this party on every year as a thank-you in advance to all the merchants who made Christmas special for families who otherwise couldn't afford one. Carly owed many of these people thanks, as well. Wide Spot was so small a town, she always had to tap the generosity of Bozeman merchants for help with Wide Spot's Giving Tree and Community Christmas Dinner. Last year, she'd wheedled a fresh turkey from each of Bozeman's grocery stores.

Tonight it seemed everyone Carly needed to talk to was half of a couple. The thought that maybe DeeDee was right—that Carly should have found a date for the party—nagged at her as she pasted on a smile for another introduction. She must be the only person in the room without a date.

As she went through the buffet line for dinner, Carly kept shooting her gaze around, looking for a table with a single person sitting at it. But she didn't see one. She ate a solitary meal, surrounded by couples.

By the time someone at the microphone began urging everyone to dance, Carly felt more alone than she ever remembered feeling. The three couples she'd shared the table with rose in unison as the band began playing.

Embarrassed to remain by herself at the table, Carly rose, too, trying to look a part of the crowd on the dance floor. The swirl of brightly dressed dancers flowed by her in a blur that she refused to attribute to the lonely tears she was fighting. The room felt colder than ever.

Without long sleeves or a dancing partner, Carly saw no reason to stay. She started toward the exit.

"Oh, no, you don't," said a man's deep voice behind her as she neared the door. A large male hand tightened around hers and turned her into his chest. "Surely you aren't trying to sneak out, are you? Before the—" he spoke in an ominous Dracula tone "—speeches?" He slid his arm behind her waist as he pulled her onto the dance floor. "You can't possibly want to miss old what's-her-name thanking the entire population of Montana individual by individual, can you?"

Giggling, Carly glided into the dance with him. "Of course I wouldn't dream of missing that," she said. "It's just so cold in here, I was going to get a sweater."

"A likely story."

"True, though," she insisted. "This dress isn't very warm."

She didn't need to tell him that most of her cold came from the inside, that until he'd asked her to dance, her loneliness had seemed about to freeze her.

"We can fix that," he said, spreading his hand over the small of her back to pull her closer. "We'll share my heat."

Warmth flowed through her as he pulled her hard to him. In fact, everything about him felt hard and warm. His deep chest, where she pressed her cheek, was covered in a soft cashmere jacket that radiated his heat. The strength in his arm around her, the powerful muscles of his thighs, moved them together in easy unison.

"Oh," she sighed, "you are warm." She snuggled closer, any resistance she might have felt overpowered by her longing for the touch of another human being.

Though she knew it was silly, Carly wanted to cling to him the way a drowning woman would grab a life preserver. She had begun to feel weirdly distant from all the twosomes at the party, as if she were invisible, or dreaming the whole thing. Closing her eyes, she let herself relax in the embrace of this strong, very real man.

Something felt not right beneath her cheek and she raised one eyelid fractionally. The word "John" met her gaze.

"John?" she murmured.

"Pardon me?"

"John," she repeated. "Isn't that your name?"

"Uh, right, one of them."

"Your name tag is pinching."

His fingers gently slipped under her cheek to remove the sticker. Carly turned her head from side to side, feeling his fingers slide caressingly over her cheek. She decided not think about who was caressing whom. Lifting her head to get a good look at him, she felt the rush of another kind of warmth.

He was gorgeous. His eyes were so dark they were almost black, made brown only by warm golden flecks deep within the irises. And their almond shape made them seem to be smiling all the time.

John crumpled his tag. "I've never liked these anyhow. How'd you manage to avoid one?"

"Put one of those sticky things on a silk dress?" Carly said, horrified.

"Bite my tongue," John said, smiling. "I'll just call you 'Silk Dress.'" His hand gently pressed her head back against his warm wool-covered chest. "It's what every other man in the room is probably calling you anyway…at least when his wife's not listening."

As Carly nestled back into his chest, she considered protesting his remark. But she'd bought the dress because of the way her long, wavy blond hair looked against the dark green, and the way the blouson top and fitted skirt shimmered when she moved. Should she protest now because the hunkiest man at the party noticed?

Instead she murmured, "My name's Carly."

John nodded, his chin moving near her head. It shocked Carly to realize that even that innocuous little movement gave her pleasure. How long had it been since she danced with a man? How long since she had let touch go beyond the impersonal? She didn't care to think about it. Instead she wriggled closer, trying to get more of her body to touch his.

Perhaps she should explain to John that she didn't act this way, she really wasn't herself tonight. Except she couldn't deny it *felt* like herself. It felt like the self she usually kept in check—the fool who thought she needed other people.

Carly snuggled closer still. It felt so good to be held this way. It didn't really matter what John thought of her, it was only one dance.

And they fit together perfectly. His unyielding arm on her waist held her firmly, securely, yet without demand. Big as his hands were, when he'd raised her cheek then urged her head back to his chest, his touch had been gentle, almost tender.

Yearning spread in Carly. She'd denied herself for *so* long. And this man, this gentle, powerful man, was reminding her of that with every move he made as he steered them together around the dance floor. She curled her right hand in close to their bodies, pulling his with it.

John's other hand moved lower on her back, exerting pressure—surely more pressure than before: she wasn't imagining that, was she?—very near her buttocks. Carly almost groaned. Shivering was the last thing on her mind now.

"Silk?" John murmured.

"Mmm?"

"The music has stopped." He tried to uncurl their hands but she resisted.

"Uh-uh," she whispered. "I don't want to stop."

"I need to stop," he said. "Or get somewhere more private."

Unwillingly, Carly opened her eyes. "Hmm?"

John gave her rear a gentle pat and straightened slightly. "I think we're supposed to eat dessert now and listen to old you-know-who."

"I'm not hungry." Carly leaned back just enough to meet his eyes.

"Really?" John's gaze filled with heat. "I'm... ravenous."

Carly raised a hand, with every intention of stroking her palm along his smooth-shaven cheek, feeling the rugged curve of his jaw, maybe even tracing a finger down the line of his beautiful straight nose, or his full square mouth.

Suddenly she realized what she was about to do in the middle of a party, and she snatched her hand back. She doubted she was blushing though; she felt too flushed already from the dance.

With reluctance, she stepped out of his arms, then wished she hadn't. Giving up the warmth of their two-ness brought the ache of loneliness back to her.

John took one of her hands to lead her to the table. "You're cold again, Silk." Concern wiped the smile from his face. "Don't you feel well?"

"I feel wonderful." She tried to control her trembles but that seemed to make them worse. She couldn't tell

John they no longer had anything to do with cold. "Just afraid of letting this lovely feeling evaporate." Her hand still in his, she turned toward the door. "I think I'll go...get my sweater after all."

John looked suspicious. "You up to your old tricks again, Silk? Sneaking out on the speeches?" He shot a glance toward the speakers' table. "I'll see you to your room."

"You don't have to," she said, though she didn't release his hand.

John nodded. "Yeah, it's really rough walking all the way up the stairs with the most beautiful woman in the room instead of—"

The mike crackled. "Would everyone take a seat for a few minutes?" boomed a woman's voice. "We just have a couple of announcements."

John rolled his eyes. "Let's get out of here." He hurried them out of the dining room.

When Carly found herself walking slowly up the wide staircase toward her room with this man, reality threatened to intrude. She stepped closer to John and, as if he knew she didn't want to think about anything else just then, he put his arm around her shoulders.

Carly leaned on him, letting herself feel nothing but the comforting strength in his body, the answering need in hers. She was lonely, it was Christmas. Hadn't DeeDee urged her to indulge herself a little?

At her door, he turned her to him, and she gazed at his warm dark eyes, his expressive mouth, wondering why he looked expectant.

A grin tilted his lips. "Got a key? Or shall I break down the door for you?"

Carly remembered where she'd put her key and

winced. "I, uh…" She fluttered a hand at her dress. "I don't have a purse for this outfit."

John raised a brow. "You're locked out?" He started to remove his coat. "You'd better wear this while I go get the—"

Carly stopped him with her hand over his. "No, I have it." Turning away slightly, she reached into her bodice and pulled the key out of her bra.

John chuckled. "Lucky key," he said, taking it from her fingers. "God, this key is hot. I thought you were shivering earlier."

"Earlier," Carly agreed quietly.

Just the feel of his hand brushing hers made her tremble now. She longed to feel close to him again, to feel his heat again.

So many emotions and sensations and needs she'd forgotten she had swirled through Carly, she couldn't make sense of her thoughts. The whole evening, brief as it was, had a dreamlike quality.

But one thing was completely clear to her. She didn't want John to leave.

He pushed open the door and held the key out to her. When she reached to take it, his fingers surrounded hers. "Better get into something warmer, Silk. So you don't get chilled again."

Carly didn't try to free her hand. "I'm much warmer now."

She looked through the open doorway and her gaze lighted on the king-size bed, softly lit by the one small lamp she'd left burning. She didn't want to go inside, to move out of the warmth she felt standing close to John.

She couldn't stop staring at the bed, so soft and warm-looking, so inviting. Carly shook her head, hoping to clear it.

What had one dance done to her? Did she really mean to turn her back on rationality and let her emotions decide something like this for her? It was so unlike her.

But tonight was unlike any other night she could remember.

Carly took the key and walked into her empty room. She turned to say goodnight to John. But she didn't close the door, didn't stand close enough to reach it. She would leave it to John to close, and to decide for himself which side of it he would be on when he did so.

"'Night,'' she said. "Thanks for seeing me to my room. Well, to the door of my room." She smiled. "I'm all safe and sound now." She let her eyes meet his, not hiding her feelings. "I'm sorry to say."

"Ah, God, Silk." John strode into the room, kicking the door shut behind him, and took her in his arms. "I hope you mean it."

He kissed her then, hard and deep, till her knees felt like half-set Jell-O. When he lifted his lips, she clung to him, breathing as hard as a long distance runner.

"I need to sit down," she said, her chest heaving.

John led her across the room and eased her down onto the edge of the bed.

Carly slumped back, sighing. All her muscles seemed to let go of the bones they supported. She relaxed totally. For now, just this once, just for tonight, she would let herself need someone. Let herself pretend it was safe to trust someone else. She took his hand and pulled him toward her.

"Silk," he said, his voice rough. "I'm right on the edge. You have about one second to change your mind and tell me to get the hell out of here." He stroked his palm down her cheek, cupping it under her chin to lift her face to his. "Not that I want you to."

"I'm getting cold again," Carly whispered. "Will you hold me while I get warm?"

"God, Silk." John's expression looked almost as if he were in pain. He stroked a hand down her arm. "I wanted you downstairs when I was standing up surrounded by other people. What do you think it will do to me to hold you in a bed?"

"And to me," Carly said. Confusion filled her, but it did nothing to temper her desire. "I don't understand this, either," she said. "I want you, too, but I don't... I mean, I never..." In the chill from John's resistance, she grabbed the quilted bedspread and pulled it over her. "I don't mean to make you...do something that feels wrong to you."

"Wrong?" John shook his head. He pulled her into his arms and lay down next to her. "Wrong? Are you crazy? But it's..."

"Fast. I know. But I...want..." Her words were turning to moans. His arms around her felt so strong, so exciting, Carly couldn't help herself. She arched against him. "I want..."

"Oh, God, so do I." John covered her mouth with his, sliding his big hand to her buttocks and hauling her hard against him.

His male reaction to their closeness swelled powerfully against her. John's lips and tongue took possession of her mouth, his hands roamed tenderly, passionately, over her body. Carly couldn't have said what was happening to her, but she agreed with John. It was right. It was *so* right.

CHAPTER TWO

CARLY woke with the curve of her body tucked into the crook of John's, his arm holding her protectively to him. She felt warm and safe and somehow...beloved.

Too bad she didn't believe it.

Gently, Carly lifted John's arm and slipped out of bed. He groaned and reached for her without waking, as if seeking her body in his sleep.

In the moonlight, Carly found their clothes heaped on the floor beside the bed. Carefully she extracted her own from the pile.

Not that she had any desire to wear the dress again. But it had cost her too much to throw away just because she'd been wearing it while she made a mistake.

Carly paused. *A mistake?* She shook her head. Actually, though her behavior last night had been quite out of character, she didn't feel as if she'd made a mistake. She wasn't racked with guilt or remorse.

Nor even fear of the consequences. John had protected her in that way, too.

No, even without the Christmas loneliness that attacked her last night, when Carly looked at John slumbering in the bed they'd shared, she didn't feel regret. Her instincts hadn't failed her: something about last night had been very, very right.

But it was over.

Quietly she dressed in the jeans and sweater she'd worn for the drive to Bozeman. She hoped the snow had

16

stopped. Four a.m. might be morning instead of night, but it was just as dark.

Still, she didn't wish to breakfast with John. To...do the morning after. To try to explain what had been different last night. Right as it had felt, it had been a magic interlude that wouldn't have happened if she hadn't let her defenses down.

She stuffed her clothes and toiletries into her overnight bag and paused at the door, staring at John another minute. Was he as charming as he'd seemed? Or would that overprotective quality become annoying in a short time?

It didn't matter, she wouldn't ever find out. Last night had been wonderful, but it was hardly the way to begin a relationship. The woman John had taken to bed wasn't Carly. When he got to know the real woman he would be disappointed. They'd simply been drawn together by overpowering sexual chemistry.

Carly sighed. Actually "overpowering" didn't begin to describe it.

Oddly, she didn't feel sad at what they might have missed. The kind of pleasure she and John had given each other was so intense, she was afraid to experience it often...or even again. She might grow to *need* it.

Unwilling to look deeper into that thought, Carly slipped quietly from the room. When she passed the desk downstairs, she dropped her key on the blotter. No one was in the darkened lobby when she left the inn.

On the drive home, she had the road to herself. In the cold, the snow crackled beneath her tires, and everything visible in the moonlight looked startlingly beautiful with its new layer of white.

Like a Christmas card, Carly thought. She hoped that thinking of Christmas would put her mind on all she had to do before December twenty-fifth, instead of on the night she'd just spent.

But it didn't work. Last night still seemed to envelope her. She wondered what other incredible things she and John would have done together if he'd awakened to find her in his arms.

When Carly got home, she ignored the phone as long as she could—perhaps three minutes. Then she called the inn and asked them to ring her room. Not because she had any desire to start a relationship with John. She had simply decided she ought to say goodbye to him in a less stark way than running out without a word.

But it didn't matter. The phone rang and rang with no answer.

Two days later, Carly dressed for her mediation appointment, still trying to put John from her mind.

Her mediation office was a converted storeroom in the back of the gift shop she ran with her mother, DeeDee. Though not large, the room had its own entrance—a necessity for giving her clients some privacy—and a big window. Sheetrock, paint, and bright curtains made the room fine for her purposes. She'd even added extra soundproofing in case her clients' voices rose too loud when tempers flared.

Carly hoped it wouldn't come to that today. A bit of that soft cocoon of pleasure she'd felt in John's arms seemed to linger around her. Too much reality would blow it away.

Blow it away forever, since without John's last name she didn't have any idea how to find him. Not that she wanted to, she hastily reminded herself.

Carly unlocked the outside door, made a pot of coffee and turned up the heat. Since she and DeeDee had agreed to buy nothing for themselves, nor waste money on frivolities, until all of Web Underbrook's debts were paid off, Carly kept the heat off in this room unless she had clients coming.

When her father died, Carly had been in her last year of college, and DeeDee had insisted that she finish. But Carly's dream of going to law school had died with her father. Not that she was unhappy with her choice of becoming a lay mediator. In many ways, it seemed to suit her nature better than litigation would have.

Carly stayed there in the gradually warming room instead of going back out to help her mother in the gift shop. Sitting in one of the captain's chairs at the round table, she tried again to straighten out her thoughts about the other night. But she couldn't.

She didn't have any thoughts about it. Only feelings, emotions that bent not at all to logic. Desires she'd long suppressed. Needs she would have said she didn't have.

Needs, hah! Carly took care of herself.

Besides, what if it turned out she did need this man she couldn't seem to get out of her thoughts? What was she going to do about it? Call that woman at United Way and pump her for information? That would be a wonderful conversation.

She and John certainly hadn't left the party together entirely unnoticed by others. And if any of those who noticed also noticed that neither of them ever came back...

Carly didn't want to fuel gossip by asking questions about the man.

Her tumbling thoughts were just presenting her with the next question—what would you do if you learned his name, call and ask him for a return engagement?—when a knock on the door saved her.

She rose to open the door and words of welcome stuck in her throat. There on the stoop was, Carly assumed, the woman who had made this appointment, Sylvia Parsons. Carly barely noticed the tall, attractive woman. Her attention was arrestingly drawn to the other party, Ms. Parsons's business partner.

John.

Stunned into silence, Carly stared at the black-brown eyes smiling at her.

"Hello," Sylvia said. "You must be Ms. Underbrook. May we come in?"

"Oh, uh, of course," Carly said, opening the door wide and stepping out of the way. "I'm Carly Underbrook, but, uh… Yes, come in. Of course. Uh, please sit down."

Oh, Lord, no, that wasn't what she should have said. She should have ended this before it began, left them on the stoop and slammed the door. But she was too stunned to know how to react, and her mediator's training took over, leading her woodenly through the motions.

Before she could stop herself, Carly had offered them chairs at the table. Feeling helplessly drawn along, she took the seat between them.

She wanted to shake her head, like a dog shaking off water. She couldn't go forward with this.

Carly cleared her throat. "I, uh…" She knew her cheeks must be red, they felt on fire. No useful words came to mind.

"Let's begin with introductions, shall we?" Ms. Parsons said.

Carly cringed inside. *She* should be the one making introductions, making these clients feel welcome. Instead she wanted to make them leave. "Uh, yes. Of course."

"I'm Sylvia Parsons," Ms. Parsons said, apparently oblivious to Carly's unease, "and this is Jonah St. John. We're partners in Jonah's Toys—I'm sure you've heard of it."

"Oh, good G— Uh, yes, I...everyone has," Carly stammered.

Jonah St. John. Dear Lord, I spent the night with Jonah St. John. She wondered how out of it she'd really been at the party not to have figured out John's real name. Except... John...half the men in the world were named "John", weren't they? How could she have guessed this "John" was attached to "Saint"?

She flashed a weak smile. "I'm Carly Underbrook. I guess I already said that."

"Repeat it as often as you want," Jonah said. "I didn't catch it the other night."

"The other night?" Sylvia said.

"Yes, Ms. Parsons." Carly decided to deal with this head-on. After all, she always began a mediation by disclosing any relationship she had with either of the parties. In so small a town, it happened frequently. "I met your partner the other night at the Christmas dance at the inn, though we never...um, we were never quite introduced. I, uh... I'm not sure I'm the one to handle this mediation for you. Since I know Joh... Mr. St. John socially, I might feel a bias."

"Oh, nonsense," said Sylvia. "We drove seventy-five miles to see you for that very reason. We know all the mediators in Bozeman too well. We don't wish to discuss our business problems with people we know socially. One dance at a Christmas party hardly qualifies you as a friend."

"Uh..." Carly wondered what one night in bed with this woman's live-in lover qualified her for. But she couldn't explain *that* to Sylvia. "Actually it was more than just a dance." She didn't meet Jonah's eyes. "I wasn't feeling, um…quite myself, and Mr. St. John was…very helpful. Kind. I felt quite…grateful."

Sylvia's eyes narrowed slightly. "We don't need to make a big deal of that," she said. "Jonah is often too kind. That's why so many people take advantage of him."

Carly bit down on her embarrassment at Sylvia's curt dismissal of her emotions. She reminded herself that Sylvia didn't know all the facts. Besides, Carly was the mediator here, *her* feelings didn't matter.

"I don't think I took advantage of him," Carly said. "But—"

"Of course not," Sylvia said. "Not if you weren't feeling well. But don't let it bother you today. I'm sure Jonah didn't think another thing about it, or he'd have mentioned it to me." She shot a glance at Jonah, whose even features showed no emotion. "Now I hope you'll agree that we can go ahead."

Carly couldn't think of a response. Of course, it didn't surprise her that Jonah hadn't "mentioned" their evening. But, rational or not, hearing that he hadn't "thought another thing about it," when she had thought of almost nothing else, hurt in a way she didn't want to acknowledge.

"We heard good things about you," Jonah said, his tone just barely humorous. "It's not easy to talk about these things to just anyone." His eyes gleamed with suppressed laughter. "Usually it takes months to know someone well enough for such…intimacy."

Carly decided she would caucus alone with Jonah later in a one-on-one and strangle him. That would solve all these problems, Sylvia's and hers.

"Of course, Mr. St. *John*."

Sylvia looked back and forth between the two of them, frowning. "Have I misread this, Jonah?" she asked. "Do you have a problem working with Ms. Underbrook?"

"On the contrary," Jonah said, without a hint of a smile. "I think this mediation will proceed—" he shot Carly an ironic glance "—as smooth as *silk*."

"Mr. St. John," Carly began, "I don't think—"

"Carly," Jonah interrupted. "Can't we use first names here?"

"Of course, but—"

"Let me explain how we chose you."

All the humor left his tone, he sounded quite serious. Carly couldn't help noting the change. It made her respond as a mediator, giving him her full attention.

"You aren't a lawyer," Jonah said. "We're in this mess because of a lawyer."

"Absolutely," said Sylvia. "We don't want any more help like that. And all the other mediators we heard anything positive about are lawyers." She folded her hands in her lap. Though the gesture seemed demure, Carly felt a profound determination coming from this woman. "It's you or no one, Carly."

Carly shut her eyes a moment, trying desperately to compose her tumbling thoughts. Jonah obviously had no intention of backing out of this now that he knew who she was. Nor would he help *her* get out of it.

Surely if she explained the situation honestly to Sylvia... Carly shuddered. She couldn't. Which left her no choice but to go forward.

She let out a deep sigh. Just moments before Jonah had arrived, she'd been assuring herself that she wouldn't see him again even if she knew where to find

him. Hadn't she? Now that she knew who he was, that
he was living with another woman, Carly was even more
sure that she would never permit herself another…
encounter with him.

It had a been a fling. A one-night thing, something
she never did, certainly never would do again.

She could put it out of her thoughts and handle this
mediation professionally. In fact, acting as mediator
would put a safe distance between her and Jonah. She
certainly couldn't have any personal contact with him
while he was a mediation client.

More than once, Carly had handled mediations when
she was very good friends with one of the parties, and
it hadn't made a difference. Surely she could handle this
one.

Carly looked up. Sylvia was looking at her oddly. The
woman was tall and very attractive. Her short dark hair
curled around her face in a way that set off her tawny
probing eyes.

Internally Carly gave in. Trying to handle the mediation would be considerably easier than trying to explain
to those catlike eyes.

"Let's begin," she said, glancing back and forth between them. "Is everyone comfortable? I can turn the
heat up—or down if you'd prefer. And I've made coffee
there." She gestured at the counter in the corner. "But
I can get you something else if you'd—"

"Maybe later," Sylvia interrupted. "I'm fine for now,
aren't you, Jonah?"

Carly glanced at him and felt her gaze catch in his.
She couldn't blink, couldn't look away.

His smile was entirely contained in those dark eyes,
no other feature moved. "No, thanks," he said, "I don't
think I need any added stimulation right now."

Carly pushed her long hair back from her face, wondering if she would get through this meeting with her sanity intact. "Very well," she said, relieved at least she didn't have to serve coffee when she wasn't sure she could keep her hands steady. "Did you read and sign the Agreement to Mediate?"

"Yes." Sylvia took both the agreements out of the briefcase she'd put on the floor. "We did, though I'm sure it will kill Jonah not to interrupt. It's his favorite way of winning a discussion."

Carly turned to him. "That's the most important rule, Jonah," she said, wanting to use his name to be sure she could say it naturally. "No matter what, we don't interrupt each other."

Jonah shook his head. "Sylvia's exaggerating. As usual."

Carly bit her lip. "These sorts of personal remarks only slow the mediation process. I'll try to eliminate them from your statements. But I don't solve this problem for you, you do understand that? I just try to help facilitate an agreement you two work out yourselves."

"I'm not sure how you can do that," Jonah said, "without making suggestions. We've been arguing about it for months and haven't come close to a solution. All we've concluded is neither of us wants to give up our rights to the business."

Carly nodded. "It may not be easy. Shall we begin?" She looked at Sylvia. "Why don't you give us your opening statement first? Explain in as much detail as you want exactly what you think the problem is."

"Oh, the problem is easy to describe," Sylvia said. "It's an answer that's difficult."

Carly simply nodded. It wouldn't do any good at this point to explain that getting to the root of the problem usually provided a solution. People who'd been arguing in circles for a long time couldn't see that.

"We're full partners in the business," Sylvia said. "In Jonah's Toys. It's his name, because he makes the toys. He's the one everyone knows about, the creative genius. But Jonah's Toys would never have become a nationally recognized company if it weren't for me. I'm the business genius." She hadn't moved while she spoke, her hands were still clasped tightly in her lap, her legs crossed, an ankle pulled behind the leg of the chair. "Jonah will admit that."

Sylvia looked to Jonah as if for confirmation. Though Carly usually didn't think it was a good idea for the parties to interrupt each other's opening statements, Sylvia seemed to need it.

She turned to Jonah. "Sylvia feels that your and her contributions to the business of Jonah's Toys are equal, that each of you brings something unique and different to the business, and that without either of you it wouldn't have done so well."

"I agree with that," Jonah said. "Completely. It's just beside the point now—"

Carly held up a palm. "Let's let Sylvia finish."

Sylvia uncrossed her legs. "When we began the business...well, not right away, but quite soon after...when the business began to get big, which was after we got out of college..."

She paused a moment, gazing out the window, as if organizing her thoughts. "Jonah and I met in college. He was making toys then on a very limited basis. Selling them to a few toy stores around Montana, to friends. He didn't earn much, barely enough to put himself through college."

She looked back to Carly, placing a fist firmly on the

chair arm. "He was making *nothing*. He hadn't any idea how good he was. That's when I took him over." Pink stained her cheeks and she gave an embarrassed little laugh. "That is, I took over the business part of his toy making."

Carly kept her gaze doggedly on Sylvia. She couldn't bear to look at Jonah this moment, to see how he felt hearing this assertive woman explain so dispassionately that she had "taken him over."

Oh, how Carly wished she didn't have to hear these things. Normally she had no trouble maintaining her neutrality. But she couldn't help thinking that Sylvia was on the wrong track if she believed she could "take over" the powerful man Carly had spent the night with.

"After college, when we could devote ourselves to the business full-time, it began to really take off." Pride sharpened Sylvia's expression. "Then, of course, when we had all that time together, we..." Her jaw clenched, but Carly couldn't tell if she was holding back angry words or tears. "We decided to sign a partnership agreement. A lawyer wrote it for us. We gave him some ideas, but he wrote it. And he didn't...we didn't see all the consequences at the time. It didn't cover everything. It didn't..." Her tawny eyes met Carly's and the anger was obvious. "It's a disaster."

Jonah was watching Sylvia, nodding his head absently as if he agreed with everything she'd said so far.

Carly tried to ignore him, but she seemed to feel him even when she wasn't looking at him or thinking about his reactions. "That's the beginning of your problem, the partnership agreement?"

"That *is* the problem!" Sylvia exclaimed.

"Why don't you try to be a little more specific?" Carly said, choosing a neutral stock phrase.

"I don't want to break up the business," Sylvia snapped. "Jonah does. And neither of us wants to let a judge decide this for us. The partnership agreement says that if one of us wants to leave the business and the other doesn't, then the one who wants to stay gets the whole business. That's me. I should have it. I should be Jonah's Toys."

Carly stared, unable to form a proper response. She could almost feel Jonah tensing as he made himself wait his turn to speak.

Unprofessionally, Carly herself wanted to respond, *Sylvia's Toys? You must be kidding.* But of course she wouldn't really take sides, no matter how she felt personally.

"I don't completely understand," she said. "What would make the two of you, after years of running a successful business, decide to break it up?"

"*I* don't want to break it up," Sylvia repeated. She pursed her delicate bow of a mouth. Finally she went on as if under duress. "Jonah has never made the business decisions, he makes creative ones. Now he wants to interfere in my bailiwick—marketing, sales, distribution. He has no expertise in those areas." She curled her fingers into a fist. "And he's ignoring mine."

"Is the partnership agreement specific about who handles what in your business?" Carly asked.

"No, I'm sorry to say." Sylvia shifted her gaze to Jonah. "But it's always been understood. We've never had any problem before—because we never stepped on each other's toes."

The look Jonah gave her held no anger. In fact, he looked so sympathetic and understanding, Carly wondered how they could have come to such a deadlock in their negotiations.

"If you both agreed about what would happen if one of you wanted to leave," Carly asked, cringing at the thought of Jonah having to give up the toy business that bore his name, "what problem still needs mediation?"

Sylvia let out an exasperated breath. "That's where the lawyer *really* screwed up. The patents to the toys are all in Jonah's name and he intends to keep them. I believe *I* will have the rights to the ones we've already sold through the company. He disagrees, of course. Says he'll take them all to the new company he'll start if I don't give in on everything. And the noncompetition clause is so vaguely written that...well, who knows what it would bind Jonah to. It's a lawsuit waiting to happen." She closed her eyes and shook her head in disgust. "Lawyers! You can see what a mess we're in."

Carly nodded. She had to agree. "It sounds as if you might have a case against this lawyer who—"

"That's exactly what we want to avoid!" Sylvia said vehemently. "Lawsuits, publicity, and probably no resolution of things for years. If ever!" She gave another gusty sigh and leaned back.

"Are you satisfied with your opening statement?" Carly asked since Sylvia seemed to be done.

Sylvia nodded curtly. "It's complete enough, I guess."

Carly turned to Jonah. "The floor is yours. Explain as much as you like, but as you do so, try to respond to the need Sylvia has expressed. She has been willing to remain unknown in your business because she knows that you realize how great her contribution is. She feels that continuing in the business together without your respect would be impossible."

Jonah regarded Carly as if he'd never seen her before. "I hadn't thought of it that way," he said. "That

Sylvia's basically anonymous. It's such a nuisance for me being known, I never realized how that could make her feel. Of course I still respect her work, it's just…''

He stretched his legs out in front of him and jammed his hands into his pockets, not looking at either woman for a moment. "I think Sylvia left out a lot of pertinent information," he said. "We both know the whole story, of course, in more detail than you have time to hear. I don't know how much of it you need to know."

"Just explain your position as thoroughly as you can," Carly said. "The more information I have, the more helpful I can be. Frequently I know something about the problem before the mediation starts. In this case, I'm completely in the dark."

Jonah raked a hand through his thick brown hair. The motion reminded Carly too intensely of the way he'd let his fingers linger in her hair the other night. A rush of emotions and sensations washed over her. She wanted to look away, to blank her mind. But she couldn't, she had to concentrate on Jonah. It was her job.

"We signed this damned partnership agreement when we decided to get married," Jonah said, irritation in his voice. His next words told her where he aimed the irritation. "That damn fool lawyer convinced us that we ought to keep work and love separate and that, if we signed a partnership agreement, our business problems would never interfere with our marriage."

Married? Carly hoped her jaw wasn't hanging all the way to her chest. It had been bad enough when she thought she'd spent the night with a man who was living with another woman. Now she found out she'd spent the night with a married man. And he with her, leaving his *wife* downstairs dancing.

Carly swallowed her protest. It had nothing to do with

her work today. It had to do with her pain at the growing realization that the other night had meant far more to her than it had to Jonah.

He stood up and paced the tiny room. "I don't think well without some movement," he said. "Do you mind?"

"It's all right with me if it's all right with Sylvia," Carly lied. In fact, she wished he'd sit down so she couldn't see the movement of muscle in his thighs and buttocks. The way his jeans fit, it was hard to miss. "At least when *you're* speaking. When Sylvia's speaking, I think you'll pay more attention if you sit still."

"Probably," he muttered. "Not that I haven't heard it all already."

"If you come into this discussion with that attitude, it'll last longer than necessary," Carly said, hoping she didn't sound as much like a stuffy old schoolmarm to them as she did to herself.

To her, the room felt so alive with emotion, she wondered how the small space could contain it all. She had to keep herself tightly reined in to keep from crying at what she was learning—or demanding that they leave. If her rigid control made her words come out a little stiff and formal, that was better than letting them see what she was really feeling.

"Right, right," Jonah said. "I'll listen. I'll listen to your version of it anyway. You don't come so cheap that I can afford to ignore you."

Carly took shallow breaths as she looked at Jonah. Surely he meant only that her fees for mediation were not low. He didn't mean, did he, that she was cheap?

Suddenly he seemed to realize how his words could have sounded. His hand made a jerky movement, as if he started to reach for her but stopped himself.

"Please go on," Carly said. "Please?"

"Yeah," Jonah said almost to himself. "Sylvia does make the business decisions. She's the one who got national distribution for my toys, even before we got out of college. I'm a rich man today because of her, I don't deny it."

He was behind Sylvia's chair when he said this and he gave her shoulder a pat. Carly tightened her grip around the arms of her chair. She didn't blink. She knew if she closed her eyes for a second, she'd picture the way that hand had looked on her skin, felt on her body... Her chest tightened as she envisioned how it would look on Sylvia's body. His wife's body.

"But that doesn't mean that I never had anything to say about how we do business." Jonah resumed his pacing. "I don't make killing toys. I don't do violence. Not in my toys, not in my life. I don't even go to violent movies." He stopped to regard Carly. "Do you know the motto of my toy business?"

"I've heard it," Carly said. "'Unbreakable Toys That Break The Rules,' isn't it?"

"Yes," Jonah said. "I've always made toys kids can use as a rebellion thing, a way to poke fun at adults. Even make fools of them. But not kill them, not kill each other. I don't do that." He shook his head. "Too many kids have to deal with real violence in their lives. I won't add to it." He put his fists on hips, looking sternly down at his wife and business partner. "That's what Sylvia wants me to do. I won't let any business with my name on it do that—no matter who's running it."

Sylvia didn't seem to feel the need for movement that Jonah did. She reminded Carly of a beautiful china doll. Carly could barely fit the two pictures together in her mind: the statuesque woman, sitting immobile and perfect in her chair, and a maker of violent killing toys for small children.

"If I'm hearing Jonah correctly," Carly said, forcing an utterly neutral tone, "he feels that whatever direction the company takes, ethics need to be part of the decision-making process. Especially this particular ethic of not adding to the violence already in children's lives."

Sylvia flicked her hand in a dismissive gesture. "Oh, that's *so* out of date," she said disdainfully. "He just has this...*thing* about children." She turned to look at him for the first time since he'd moved beside her chair. "Honestly, Jonah, I'm surprised you haven't impregnated a dozen women by now."

Jonah put a hand on the back of her chair. "One would be enough for me, Sylvia, you know that."

A good mediator, Carly chastised herself as she sat silent, her eyes rounding into saucers, would have cut into that exchange, paraphrased Sylvia's words to take the heat and emotion out of them before she let Jonah respond. But how did you take the emotion out of a married couple discussing children?

Carly wanted to run from the room. Send DeeDee back in to inform them that Carly would be unable to handle their case. Then go up to her bedroom and cry for an hour at least.

Instead she said, "Can I get anyone a cup of coffee? I could use one."

As she watched powdered creamer swirl into the black liquid, the only thought in Carly's churning brain was, *Thank God, he used a condom.*

CHAPTER THREE

AFTER serving coffee, Carly returned to her chair, determined to treat these two people as she would any other couple. Any fantasies she might have harbored about "John" the last two days—not that she'd actually dignify those fleeting thoughts enough to call them "fantasies"—had turned out as substantial as fresh powder on a ski hill. Great fun for a day, but gone before you knew it.

John didn't even exist. Jonah did. He was a married man, planning babies with his wife.

"I don't think we're getting to the core of your problem," Carly said, quickly distracting herself from…the baby subject. "Sylvia, have you always thought Jonah should incorporate violence into his toys? Or has a change taken place in the business that makes you think it's necessary now?"

"I've always thought he was a little overboard on the subject," Sylvia said, "even with his history."

"We're not going to discuss that here, Sylvia," Jonah interrupted. "We agreed, it has nothing to do with this dispute."

Sylvia regarded him stonily for a moment then gave Carly a look that clearly meant, "Men!" "He's irrational on the subject."

Carly turned to Jonah but he didn't wait for her to speak.

"I'm not irrational and it's not relevant." He glared at his partner. "Move on, Sylvia."

34

Jonah's cold, final tone hit Carly like a fist in the solar plexus. The night at the inn, she'd hidden nothing from Jonah; she'd revealed things about herself she'd kept private for years. Now his adamant refusal to allow some secret from his past to be mentioned in front of her made her realize again how little the other night must have meant to him. She couldn't talk, she just looked expectantly at Sylvia.

Sylvia let out a long-suffering sigh. "We've always done so well, it never mattered before. But now Jonah wants to move into CD-ROM games. He thinks he can take one of our old *board* games—" she said the words as if board games were a place to walk the dog "—The School Zone, and turn it into a CD-ROM game. He actually thinks kids in this day and age will buy it without excitement and danger! Weapons and killing don't bother kids, they love all that gore." Finally Sylvia was putting emotion in her voice. "It's too…risky."

"Gory games are risky?" Carly asked, confused.

"The high-tech game market is risky. We can't even begin to enter that market—which we know *nothing* about—without a huge investment. It's much too much money to venture unless we come into the market with something we know kids like." Sylvia leaned back in her chair and lowered her eyes, as if exposing so much feeling embarrassed her.

Carly turned to Jonah, surprised to see an angry frown on his face. He clearly wanted to respond. She had to dampen his annoyance before she let him speak.

"If I understand Sylvia, she's not insisting on violence *per se*. But you want to take the business in a new direction without a level of security she feels comfortable with. Is there a way you can satisfy her need and still accomplish what you want?"

"No." Jonah's glare softened slightly. "Business involves risk." He aimed his gaze at Sylvia. "We've always done well doing things our way, not following the herd. My toys sold because of their originality, but it was *always* a risk, Sylvia. Now we can either stagnate or move on—but we have to go on the way we got here. Sticking to our principles. I can't do something I find morally reprehensible, even if it'd make millions."

Carly swallowed. How dare he speak of morals and principles when he had committed adultery just two nights ago? With an effort, she pushed the thought from her mind.

"If I'm reading Jonah correctly," she said to Sylvia, "he thinks this isn't the first risk you've taken in your business, and that not making the new toys would be a greater risk than playing it safe."

"Exactly," Jonah interrupted.

Carly shook her head at him. "Please let Sylvia answer now."

Sylvia paused as if thinking that over. But the muscles in her forearms flexed as she clenched her fists tighter. "Jonah, this goes far beyond any risk we've ever taken. We'd need new people, a new factory, new contacts, new distributors." Her voice rose. "We don't know anything about the market. But we know what's on the shelves. And what we see is bloody games grabbing all the market." Her hand shook when she reached for her coffee and she put the mug back on the table without taking a sip. "*You* wouldn't have to do it, Jonah. You could make the game *your* way, then the programmers we'll need to hire could add the violence."

"No!" Jonah roared before Carly could intercede.

She held a palm toward him. "Before you give Sylvia a flat refusal, try to answer her concern that you will

bankrupt the business by not taking seriously her analysis of the new market you want to enter.''

Jonah stretched his long legs out and slumped in his
chair. ''I'll buy you out, Sylvia. Take half the available
cash. If you invest it wisely, which I know you would,
you can live on it the rest of your life. And I'll give you
twenty percent of the net for as long as I own the business. No risk for you, no more arguing. No question of
who owns the business.''

Jonah's offer seemed so reasonable, Carly caught herself almost nodding in agreement. ''Could Jonah's offer
alleviate your fear, Sylvia? Your future would be assured, and if the new toys do well, you'd still share in
the profits from them. Do you have problems with this
offer?''

''Problems? Of *course* I have problems with it. I don't
want to leave the business. I created it. It's mine as much
as Jonah's. Now he wants to push me out. For all I
know, he's ready to replace me with some bimbo who'll
do just as he asks, without question.'' She looked across
the table at Jonah, her tawny eyes bright with hurt. ''Is
that what this is all about, Jonah? Have you found a
woman who'd just adore to have your babies?''

Carly gawked in confusion. How could Sylvia speak
that way of her husband having children with another
woman? Surely Carly must have misunderstood something.

''Please help me out,'' she said, directing her question
to Jonah so Sylvia could have a moment to calm herself.
''I thought you said you two were married. Surely, you
wouldn't—''

''No.''

Jonah's eyes held hers, warm with sardonic humor.
He must read in Carly's expression the rush of relief she

felt at his answer. Jonah wasn't married. She hoped she could keep her voice impartial…if she ever thought of what to say next. His lips twitched slightly at her discomfiture. Didn't Sylvia notice? Carly prayed not.

"We were engaged once," Jonah explained. "But we decided we had an irreconcilable difference. I want children, Sylvia doesn't. We couldn't see a way around that. But we remained…friends and business partners."

Even if she'd never met Jonah before—"Met?" Is that what she and Jonah had done the other night?— Carly would have agreed with *that* decision. Children were such a basic issue for a marriage. She turned to Sylvia, mostly to keep herself from asking Jonah… What do you mean "friends"? Are you still living together?

"Jonah believes that you two mutually agreed to end your engagement. That you were both comfortable with the choice and have remained friends." Carly watched Sylvia's eyes, trying to read her reaction. "Yet you seem to have some unresolved anger over it. Would you like to go into that?"

"Of course I'm angry," Sylvia snapped, directing her annoyance at Jonah. "You pushed me out of our relationship, just like you're trying to push me out of the business now. For the same reason—I didn't live up to your exalted standards."

Jonah shifted in his chair, obviously wanting to respond to Sylvia's statement, to disagree with it. His dark eyes glistened with disapproval. Did he think Carly was treading in areas that should be left alone? He'd cut her off before when his past came up. These sorts of discussions often dredged up old resentments and hurts. But usually that helped work out the current problem.

Carly took in a long breath. "Sylvia thinks that you are ignoring her valuable contribution to the business.

She feels unsafe, as if you can push her out at will, despite your partnership agreement. She believes you pushed her out of your relationship without taking her feelings into account, simply your own. Now you are doing the same thing in the business by ignoring her deep emotional commitment to it, one that goes far beyond money.''

Carly glanced at Sylvia. Usually she would have tried to help her clients resolve their old hurt before going on to the problem at hand. But in this case, she wasn't sure she could discuss their intimate relationship without getting entangled with her own mixed-up feelings about Jonah. So she had tried to tie Sylvia's personal feelings about Jonah into her feelings about the business in one step. Carly wasn't sure she'd been entirely successful.

''Is that about the way you feel, Sylvia?'' she asked.

Sylvia had returned to her doll-like pose. ''Yes, that's right.''

Her stomach clenching, Carly swiveled her head to Jonah. ''Can you comment on Sylvia's need for greater security? To have her efforts appreciated? To feel she's being considered?''

A strange look passed over Jonah's features as he looked at his former fiancée. ''Is that true, Sylvia? You think I broke off our engagement…unilaterally?''

Sylvia nodded. ''Yes, Jonah, you did. I wouldn't have.'' She looked down at her hands. ''I wouldn't still. And now you don't even want to see me at work anymore. I can't…'' Her voice broke. ''I only get to see you at work, Jonah, I can't bear to give that up. I…love you.''

Carly couldn't find words to rephrase Sylvia's emotional declaration. Her mind had locked in on Sylvia's *other* words—that she saw Jonah *only* at work. Her

stomach fluttered. Surely that had to mean—didn't it?—
that Sylvia and Jonah didn't live together.

"God, Sylvia," Jonah muttered in Carly's silence.
"You never told me that. You were so adamant about
not having children. You were the one who said it was
insane to get married feeling the way we did about that.
I didn't ignore your feelings—I let them end our engagement."

"I didn't stop loving you, Jonah." Sylvia kept her
eyes on her clasped hands. "I always thought we
would...work things out."

Carly didn't intercede this time. She knew that she
shouldn't. Sometimes her clients got to issues they
hadn't discussed in years, or ever, and inserting herself
between them at such a time could slow the reconcilia-
tion.

But she wanted to, she wanted to scream at these two
people to stop it, to forget the deep emotional commitment they had to each other, which they were obviously
rediscovering before Carly's eyes. She bit down on her
reaction, knowing it was ridiculous. Jonah had known
Sylvia for years, had started a business with her, lived
with her, been engaged to her.

He'd only spent one night with Carly. Why couldn't
she remember that? Quit wishing for another such
night—and a bunch of days in between when they could
really get to know each other. She pressed her fingertips
to her temples, repeating internally, *It was a one-night
stand, it was a one-night stand.* No wonder her parents
had warned against such flings. They caused too much
pain to the unwary.

Jonah stood and walked around the table to Sylvia.
Reaching down, he took her hand and helped her to her
feet. "I think we'd better talk about this between our-

selves now.'' He took their coats from the rack and held Sylvia's for her. "You've helped us a lot, Carly. But I think we need to talk alone now.''

"Oh, Jonah," Sylvia said. "We've been talking alone for months."

"Yes, but I didn't know how you felt about all this," he said. "We'll come back if we need to. Isn't that a reasonable way to approach this, Carly? We don't need to do it all in one day." He waited for her gaze to meet his, and she read concern there. For her? For Sylvia? "Besides, you look a little done in, as if maybe you're getting a headache or something."

"A little," Carly lied. In fact, she was *totally* done in, and it had nothing to do with a headache. "But I can go on if Sylvia wants—"

"No, that's all right," Sylvia said. She pressed against Jonah. "If Jonah wants us to talk alone now, that's all right. We'll make another appointment when we need to. When is the best time for you?"

"Oh, I can usually make the time whenever it's convenient for you." Carly stood. "Except the end of this week. Thursday or Friday. My mother and I give a Christmas party, kind of like that one the other night. It's this Saturday, and I need to get ready for it."

"How on earth do you fit all those people in here?" Sylvia asked.

"Well, of course, it's on a much smaller scale," Carly said. "But the party has the same purpose, to thank everyone who's going to help with the Christmas charities here in Wide Spot. Well, to thank them and to get them to sign up." She chuckled. "It's easier to get them to sign up after a cup of my mother's famous nog."

Jonah nodded, a sad little smile playing over his lips.

"Yeah, a couple of nogs will do wonders in releasing inhibitions."

Carly flushed hot from her toes to the top of her head. "You're invited, you know," she said, desperate to change the subject. "We always send an invitation to your company, but I guess you get too many."

"You have no idea," Sylvia said, turning to the door. "And they're all from people who want something."

"Bingo," said Carly, hoping such an admission would keep them from even considering her invitation. "I admit it. We'd love a donation of toys from you. But donation or not—" her eyes flitted away from Jonah's penetrating gaze "—you're welcome to come to the party." She hoped Sylvia didn't hear the insincerity in her voice.

"We'll talk about it," Jonah said, putting out his hand to shake. He clasped Carly's and squeezed gently. "Thanks, Carly, you've helped us a lot."

"I don't think we got very far," Carly said, trying to disengage her hand. The feel of his skin touching hers was sending memory signals to too many places in her body. She couldn't think straight. "Call me if you need anything else."

"Count on it," Jonah assured her, giving her hand one last squeeze.

Carly leaned against the wall till the door closed behind them, then slumped into a chair, trembling from head to foot.

Saturday night, Carly dressed in a one-piece, form-fitting dark green velour suit. She'd made the Santa's elf costume the first year she and her mother put on this party. She'd also made DeeDee a Santa suit out of red sweatshirt material, with the fuzzy side out.

DeeDee knocked on Carly's open door and entered without waiting for a response. "Ready, dear?" she asked. Turning sideways to the full-length mirror, she grimaced. "I look more like Santa every year. Remember the first year, when I had to wear a pillow to make this thing fit?" She patted her stomach. "And my hair almost matches the beard now." She sighed.

Carly looked at her plump, gray-haired mother. Her light blue eyes and pink cheeks looked adorable with the costume. "You look as cute as ever. Besides, the first year you wore that was right after Daddy died. Of course you were thin. You were *too* thin. You look much better now."

"Oh, sure," DeeDee laughed. "You hear ads like that all the time on TV. Try our something-or-other, it'll put lots of cute pounds on you. People would line up to buy it."

Carly laughed with her. "Is Tommy coming tonight?"

"Of course," DeeDee said. "He pretends to believe that if we get tired enough of entertaining him here, I'll marry him just to get him to go home."

"Well, I won't get tired of him," Carly said, her voice stilted as she held her eyes wide to apply mascara. "But he's right, you should get married."

"That sounds a little odd coming from someone who hasn't dated in five years."

"It's different for me, Mom. I, uh…" Carly dusted on blusher while she tried to come up with a response that wouldn't draw them into another analysis of Carly's nonexistent love life right before a party. "I've got plenty of time. But you aren't getting any younger, you know."

"Tommy said exactly the same thing last night,"

DeeDee said. "Do the two of you plan these campaigns together?"

"Maybe we should."

"You know we agreed when your dad died, that we would work together to pay off all his debts," DeeDee said. "I'm not going to leave you to handle that alone."

"Marrying Tommy wouldn't change that." Carly unfastened her hair from the tortoiseshell clasp that held it away from her face and fluffed it out. "You could still work here as much as you do now, Mom. You'd just have—"

"I know what I'd have," DeeDee said, patting Carly's cheek. "So don't worry any more about me, please. You worry too much about everyone but yourself. Now if you're ready, let's go downstairs."

"I'll be right down."

Carly gave herself a cursory glance in the mirror and left her room. As she descended the narrow stairs from the apartment, her subconscious pushed up the thought that she would have taken more trouble with her appearance if she'd believed Jonah would attend this party. But her rational mind assured her—for the six hundredth time?—that she didn't want him to come.

As long as he and Sylvia were her mediation clients, Carly couldn't see Jonah on any other basis. She had spent the past three days consciously keeping herself so busy with arrangements for the party that she hadn't had time to think about Jonah. Well, not much anyway.

Which left her with an assortment of very mixed-up feelings that she had no idea how to straighten out. What did she feel for Jonah St. John? What did he feel for Sylvia? And most consuming, had Jonah and Sylvia moved back in together? Were they engaged again? Sleeping together?

Once again, Carly forced off these thoughts. It took more effort to do so each time she thought of him.

As the guests began to arrive, Carly tried to ignore the pain that hit her every year when she first saw her family's Christmas decorations displayed commercially. Practically every ornament on the tree and around the shop came from Carly's former life.

They reminded her forcefully of the happy, secure childhood she'd had in Portland, Oregon, with the father she'd adored, who'd adored her, who'd always got her everything she needed and most of what she wanted. They'd been well-to-do then, beyond comfortable.

What a shock when she and DeeDee had learned that their security didn't exist, it was all based on massive debt. In one horrible three-day period—beginning with Daddy's auto accident and ending with the will reading—Carly had learned that she could rely on no one but herself. Thank heavens DeeDee's parents had just retired and had agreed to sell the gift shop to their daughter for a reasonable price over an extended period. Otherwise she and DeeDee would have...

Carly didn't know. Moved under an overpass? She shuddered, not wanting to think about it.

As she turned away from the beautiful Christmas tree that dredged up these feelings, Carly's eyes widened into perfect *O*'s. Standing at the front door with DeeDee was...Jonah St. John. DeeDee took his coat and gestured him toward the buffet table where Carly was serving "fog"—her mother's special Christmas punch.

Jonah smiled as he approached. "Merry Christmas," he said. "I can see you're delighted I took you up on your invitation."

"Of course I am, Jonah," Carly said. "Christmas is for everyone."

"I'm glad you feel that way," he said, giving her a smile she didn't quite believe, "because I'm not leaving. Not without some answers."

Carly handed a cup of punch to the man next to Jonah, her hand nearly steady. "Punch?" she asked weakly.

"I'm not much into these sweet drinks," he said, "but your mother insisted I try it."

Carly poured him a cup, splashing a bit on her hand. "If you're driving all the way back to Bozeman, I should get you something weaker. Coffee maybe."

"I'm staying in Wide Spot," Jonah said.

"Oh." Carly looked around to see if Sylvia had come with him.

"I came by myself." Jonah leaned across the table, lowering his voice. "Carly, we need to talk. *Alone.*"

Carly couldn't, here in the middle of a Christmas party, "talk" to Jonah. Not the way he obviously meant—about the night they'd met. He probably wanted to begin the discussion with all those questions Carly didn't know how to answer, like why she'd acted so differently that night.

She changed the subject. "Sylvia probably didn't come because she was afraid I'd spend the party trying to get a donation out of her."

Jonah straightened, keeping his voice neutral. "She *is* the one who usually has to fend off such requests. I don't even answer the phone, except under duress."

"I knew her voice sounded familiar," Carly said, suddenly remembering. "I've talked to her on the phone... begging for toys." She shook her head ruefully. "No wonder she didn't want to come, she knows how persistent I can be."

Jonah put his still untouched mug on the table and stepped around to Carly's side to get out of the way of the line of people wanting a drink. "Don't worry about it, she's very thick-skinned." He shrugged. "I'd probably still be giving them all away if it weren't for her."

Jonah stood so close, Carly felt his warmth. She couldn't concentrate on pouring punch when she wanted to discover again the feel of the hard muscles beneath his soft blue sweater. Horrified, she realized her hands had instinctively moved toward him. She disguised the movement by waving at some friends coming in the door.

She tried to remember what he'd been saying. "Giving your toys away doesn't sound very businesslike." She swallowed. "I guess it's a good thing you have her help."

"It's more than help," Jonah said. "As she told you the other day, when I met her I was sitting on a gold mine and didn't know it. I'd probably have gone on letting people take advantage of me forever if it weren't for her."

Carly heard a change of tone in his voice. More than that, his expression changed, hardened. In fact, even his stance changed, as if tension had swept down his spine.

Before she could respond, Tommy joined them and offered to help serve. Carly introduced the two men and gratefully gave up the ladle. She shot her gaze around, wondering if she could get away with excusing herself and hiding upstairs in the apartment till Jonah got bored and left.

He must have read her mind, for he took her arm above the elbow and led her close to the fire. Her velour suit was not the warmest of her clothes, and the heat felt wonderful. Carly turned her back, warming herself.

Jonah chuckled. "You look like a green cat," he said as she arched. His dark eyes roamed over her, looking as predatory as any tomcat's. "Why'd you leave without saying goodbye, Carly?"

Unable to meet his determined gaze, she straightened and turned away from him, ostensibly to hold her hands over the fire. In fact, her sweaty palms didn't need more heat. Nor did her flushed cheeks. "I thought you were explaining how you let people take advantage of you in college," she said brightly.

She felt Jonah's glare burning into her, though she didn't look up from the crackling flames. Finally he let out a quiet oath.

"Yeah, right," he muttered. "I gave away a lot of toys, and when I sold them, I didn't ask much."

"Who'd you give toys to?" Carly asked.

"Well, my sisters," Jonah said. "They baby-sat a lot and took the toys with them to make their jobs easier. And a preschool back in my hometow—"

"Whoa," Carly interrupted. "Surely you don't think your own sisters were taking advantage of you?"

"Well, not them," Jonah said. "I always made toys for them. I wouldn't take their money. But Sylvia thought…" He frowned. "Damn it, Carly, I don't want to talk about this stuff tonight. I want to talk about you. Me. Us."

Carly looked nervously over her shoulder, relieved to see DeeDee on the other side of the shop where she couldn't possibly have heard Jonah's words over the noise from other guests. However, though she couldn't hear, DeeDee's blue eyes sparked with curiosity at Jonah's obvious interest in Carly.

Carly wanted to groan, thinking of the third degree DeeDee would give her later. "There is no 'us,'" she snapped.

"There will be, if I have anything to say about it."

He toasted her with the cup of punch he'd held while they talked. "To an us." He took a sip. "Wow. What's in this?"

Carly grinned at his reaction, one most people had when they first tasted DeeDee's fog. "An old family secret she won't give away, not even to me till..." She closed her mouth. Jonah didn't need to know DeeDee planned to give her the recipe on her wedding day.

"Potent," Jonah said.

"Too true," Carly said. "That's why Mom and I don't drink at the party, and we always get a few other nondrinkers designated, too. So we can drive anyone home who needs it. You did say you were staying over?"

"Yeah." Jonah leaned a hand on the mantel over Carly's shoulder. "I walked up here from the motel. You may have to carry me home." He leaned closer. "At least we could talk there without you acting like everyone in the room is listening." His breath swirled over her ear, sending rushes of pleasure and memories of ecstasy through her. "They don't care what we're saying, Silk. We do. Let's go."

Carly closed her eyes and forced herself to step away. "Jonah, please. Everyone will think there's something between us."

"They'll be right." He took her elbow. "Where's your coat?"

Carly freed her arm from his grasp. "There can't be."

"Can't?" Jonah asked. "Carly, I'm not asking you to spend the night." He grinned suggestively. "Not that I'd mind if you did."

She shook her head. "Jonah, I can't go off alone with you like that, not while I'm mediating a dispute between you and your partner. You feel strongly about ethics—

understand mine. Can you imagine a greater conflict of interest?"

"I hope to hell it's a conflict you already feel," Jonah growled. He put his cup on the mantel, freeing his hands to grab Carly's shoulders and turn her toward him. "Don't tell me the other night was S.O.P. for you. I won't believe it."

"S.O.P.?" Carly murmured, wishing he'd take his hands off her so she could think more clearly.

"Standard operating procedure."

"Of course not," she whispered heatedly. "I never do that."

"Never but once," Jonah corrected her. "It's not my style, either, in case you're curious."

"Is that because—" No! She bit off her words. She wouldn't ask him here about his relationship with Sylvia.

Her gaze danced around the room, avoiding Jonah's. She was dismayed to note all the meaningful looks they were getting, especially from DeeDee. Carly shrugged her shoulders, removing his hands.

"I'm glad to hear that about you," she said, "but I guess I hadn't given it a lot of thought because I was so sure I would never repeat it. That's why I left, Jonah. Because the woman I was that night and the woman I usually am…are complete opposites." She looked at him, asking with her eyes for him to believe her. "And during mediation, there's just no way—"

"Crap!" Jonah said, a deep frown creasing his brow. "Forget the mediation."

"Forget it?" Carly said. "How do you think Sylvia would react to that? You *did* say you wanted to avoid a lawsuit."

"I do," Jonah said. "I will."

"You never know what will happen in court, Jonah,"

Carly said. "What if Sylvia ended up with the toy business? That's not worth—"

"There's no way I'm going to give up my business," Jonah said adamantly.

"I can't be part of increasing your risk that might happen," Carly said.

"Don't worry about it." Jonah lifted one shoulder in a shrug. "We'll find another mediator. Bozeman's full of them."

"But Sylvia doesn't want to go to someone you know. Neither do you, you said so." Carly shook a finger at him. "Look how uncomfortable you got the other day when the conversation turned personal."

"Is *that* what you think?" Jonah looked at her as if she'd grown another head.

"Yes," Carly said. "Isn't that why you left? So you could talk alone with—"

"Silk," Jonah interrupted, his voice gentle. "I left because Sylvia's—" his tone turned cynical "—phony declaration of love upset the hell out of you. Do you think I couldn't tell?"

"Oh, I was perfectly fine," Carly lied. But her honest heart did a small flip-flop at the thought that Jonah had left so abruptly to protect her.

He stroked his index finger softly down her cheek. "Your face is as easy to read as headlines in a newspaper."

Carly opened her mouth and shut it while she regained her composure. Jonah's soft words and touch sent her thoughts tumbling illogically. "I'm the mediator—my feelings shouldn't matter."

"They matter to me," Jonah said. "You're not the only mediator in the state. Sylvia and I will find another somewhere."

"Jonah, that would be almost worse." Carly stepped away as he reached for her hand. "You switch mediators in the middle of negotiation to *date* me? Just when you and Sylvia have a chance to get back tog—"

"You're good, Silk, but you're not that good," Jonah interrupted. "Don't believe everything you heard the other day. Sylvia only loves—"

"Don't," Carly said, holding a palm toward him. "Don't tell me things I should only hear from the two of you together." She let out a deep sigh. "I knew it was a mistake to go forward the other day. Jonah, I tried to get out of it, you know I did. But I was so flustered I...didn't insist hard enough. And..."

Jonah let out an oath. "And I wouldn't let you off the hook."

"Right," Carly said. "Now I have a professional commitment to you *and* Sylvia. No matter what mediator you go to. Until you're *both* satisfied, I can't have a personal relationship with either of you."

"Just a damn minute here," Jonah said, his voice guttural with irritation. "Are you actually telling me that you won't see me until I get Sylvia's...permission?"

"Well, I wouldn't say 'permission.'"

"If I'd had one damn clue," Jonah said angrily, "that you wouldn't see me until I resolved everything with Sylvia, I'd have been out of there in a second."

"It's too late for that now," Carly said.

"Damn it, Carly, I want to see you again." Jonah's voice came out husky with frustration. "And if you're honest, you'll admit you want to see me, too."

Carly ran her tongue over her lips that felt suddenly dry. "I don't...the other night...I'm not sure about what we..."

"You were sure when it was happening." Jonah's

smile softened, turning sexy. "Me, too, God knows. It may not be the way you usually start a...relationship, but it was real, Silk. For both of us. Don't try to pretend it didn't happen."

Carly knew she was blushing furiously. She wished she had Jonah's olive skin that surely hid any blushing he'd ever done.

Without looking, she was sure DeeDee's gaze had locked in on them like a beacon. The background sounds of Christmas music and party conversation seemed to have softened into a quiet hum. Carly feared Jonah's words were reaching everyone in the room.

She faced the fire, hoping her pink cheeks would seem to come from its heat. "I didn't mean that. I wouldn't try to pretend that you weren't everyth... Well, that we didn't have an incred—" She stuttered to a halt.

Jonah's grin got broader, but he said nothing to help her out. "Yes? Do go on, Silk. I'm fascinated."

"The other night was...as you said. Not standard. It was out of the ordinary." She met his laughing gaze squarely. "One of a kind, not to be repeated."

"Not?" he said. "Want to bet on that?"

"Jonah, *please*!" she begged. "Mediation is my livelihood. I can't risk it. And I don't want...to do that again with...a stranger. You still are, you know. Once was... Well, it just happened. Repeating it would... It would change the way I feel about myself."

Jonah's expression softened. "It wouldn't change the way I feel about you, Silk, because I didn't believe you were the one-night-stand type anyway. Do you really think all that happened between us was great sex?"

"No, of course not," Carly said hurriedly, keeping her voice as low as possible. "Or it wouldn't have happened. But I can't do that again or that *is* what it would be. I hardly know you. I didn't even know your full name. And now I...like when you talk about your sisters—I don't even know how many you have. I don't know where you grew up, how you really feel about Sylvia.'' She lowered her lashes. ''How we really feel about each other.''

Jonah gave a long-suffering sigh. ''You've got to give us a chance to find those things out. We can't do that in mediation sessions in the presence of my business partner, who, trust me, is nothing more to me than that.''

''You should have thought of that,'' Carly said.

Jonah didn't swear but he made an angry noise that sounded like a swallowed oath.

Carly turned up a palm. ''Jonah, you just stumbled across me again. Why all the urgency?''

''Are you nuts?'' Jonah demanded. ''I was looking for you, but I was trying to be discreet. For *your* sake.'' He curled a finger under her chin and lifted her gaze to his. ''You don't think I'm asking for another one-night thing, do you? I want *innumerable* nights. And days, too.'' He gave her a forthright grin. ''Starting now.'' He ran his hand softly down her arm, forcing a little sigh of pleasure from her throat. ''You're just the elf here, let Santa handle it.''

Carly considered kicking him in the shin, but the soft leather elf boots she wore didn't lend themselves to inflicting pain on the kickee...just the kicker.

''I have work to do tonight,'' she said stiffly. ''I can't just leave it all for my mother. Please don't make it hard for me.''

''You win, Silk,'' Jonah said. ''I can wait.'' He glanced around at the other guests and a smile curved his mouth. ''While you're doing your Christmas thing, maybe I'll get to know your mother better. Maybe I can get *her* approval to see you during mediation.''

Carly cringed internally, knowing her mother would quiz Jonah unmercifully…and probably know more about him in ten minutes than Carly knew in three meetings. ''You won't get *my* approval, Jonah,'' she said one more time. ''Please quit asking.''

She started to move away, when Jonah grabbed her wrist and spun her back to him. ''Hey, Silk,'' he said. ''Did you get the mistaken idea from listening to Sylvia that I let women boss me around?''

''No, indeed,'' Carly said. ''Quite the reverse. You're sensitive to her feelings, I admit. But you always seem to do exactly what you want.''

''I'm glad you realize that,'' Jonah smiled. ''Because what I want now, Silk, is you.''

CHAPTER FOUR

CARLY could feel Jonah watching her as she circulated
through the rooms, explaining about the sign-up sheets
for the different Christmas charities. She tried to speak
to everyone. After all, the main reason for the party was
to get people to volunteer.

Carly couldn't, all on her own, run the Giving Tree,
the Christmas Tree Roundup *and* the Community
Christmas Dinner. Nor could she and her mother afford
it.

So she had to urge people to sign up, just as many of
them had done last year. That's why she and DeeDee
had the party when they did, the weekend after
Thanksgiving, before people got so overwhelmed by
their own Christmas concerns that they didn't have time
for others.

Finally Carly returned to the buffet table, starved. She
was filling a plate when she heard Jonah's voice behind
her.

"Why don't you just go to the North Pole and see if
Santa has an opening?" he said.

Carly turned, plate in hand. "Have you eaten,
Jonah?" she asked sweetly. "You're more than welcome, you know. Even if you have no intention of helping."

"Helping, too?" Jonah asked. "I thought you just
wanted me to donate toys." He looked down at the sign-
up sheets laid out across the table. "Where's the page
for that, by the way. I don't see one."

Carly pointed at the Giving Tree sheet. "Right there, down at the bottom where it says 'Donations.'"

Jonah looked where she pointed but made no move to pick up the pen. "I'm not Scrooge," he said, "but we can't donate toys to every little group that asks, or we won't have any left to sell. I'm not sure where our donations stand this year."

Carly raised her brows. That must be one of those business decisions Jonah left to Sylvia. She wondered if he realized how hard it was to get toy donations out of that woman.

"I think you've been Scrooge for so long, you don't see it anymore." She took a bite of her ham. "Do you know how a Giving Tree works?"

He shook his head. "Now why would Scrooge bother to learn about something that sounds so intrinsically unprofitable?"

"Very funny, Ebenezer," Carly said.

"Okay, okay," Jonah said. "How's it work?"

"Families who can't afford the Christmas presents their kids want make out a list," Carly said. "I give each family a number, so no one knows who they are. Then we write the lists on cards and hang them from the tree. People who can afford it, take a card and buy the gifts requested."

"How do you keep people who could buy their own gifts from putting their names on the tree to save money?" Jonah asked as he led her toward a chair by the tree.

"Oh, how cynical," Carly said to his back. "No one would do that. Or almost no one. You can't imagine how embarrassing it is for people to have to ask for help. Most of them would never do it for themselves, they only do it for their kids."

Jonah sat on the arm of her chair. "Yeah, you're probably right about that. I'd have a hard time asking for charity."

"I understand it better than most," Carly said. "When my father died a few years ago, I learned how painful it is in our commercial culture to find out you have nothing." No longer hungry, she put her plate on the windowsill behind her. "I couldn't even meet my best friends for lunch or shopping anymore. I was terrified they'd offer to pick up the check out of pity."

Jonah frowned. "Did you give them a chance?"

"I couldn't." Carly shook her head. "I'd put my trust in one person all those years—and learned too late my security was just a…a…" She fluttered her hand. "An illusion. I couldn't expect more from my friends than my own father."

"So you quit calling them."

"Yes," Carly said shortly. "It's not that I changed… inside. I just learned that real security means relying on myself."

Jonah put his hand on her shoulder, massaging gently. She felt relaxation start under his palm and spread down her spine. She shrugged his hand off, sure her reaction would be obvious to anyone looking.

"Sometimes, Silk," Jonah said, "it's okay to lean on someone else. Other people lean on you. Look at all this stuff you do for your town."

"I just want everyone to understand that someone in need can be just as fine a person as…" She looked at the dark eyes gazing at her. "As a wealthy owner of a toy business."

"Touché," Jonah said. "I don't claim to be a good person because of my business. Just a lucky one."

"Then why aren't you willing to share a little of that

luck?'' Carly persisted. ''When parents make out these lists for the Tree, we tell them to put down exactly what their kids want, even the brand names if it matters to the child. We want to give these kids their real Christmas wishes—just like kids in families who have more. Many times there just isn't a cheap substitute.''

Jonah nodded. ''Absolutely. That's what makes my business so successful.''

''But your toys are very expensive,'' Carly went on. ''A lot of people can't afford to take the cards with Jonah's Toys listed.'' She grabbed his hand. The rush she felt reminded her what a bad idea that was, and she quickly let him go. ''That's why we'd like a donation of toys from you. Just some Disobedient Dollies for the little kids and that handheld video game for the older ones.''

''Hey, no problem,'' Jonah said, his tone ironic. ''Just our two most popular games of the season. Sylvia will love the idea.''

Carly rolled her eyes. ''Did anyone ever tell you that you think too much about money? You said you used to give half your toys away. What changed you?''

Jonah frowned down at her, but not as though he was angry. More as though he was thinking over her words. ''I guess you can say I learned my lesson—at least in business. The hard way.''

Carly was surprised by how brisk and businesslike Jonah's voice became when he spoke about his company. ''What do you mean?''

''We began to get so successful,'' Jonah said, ''it became awkward charging some people one price and others another or nothing at all.''

''Wasn't it awkward telling friends you were going to charge them for something they used to get for free?''

"Probably," Jonah said. "Sylvia handled that part of it. But I'm not sure I'd call them 'friends.' We never saw some of those people again." He turned up a palm. "So did they ever like me? I don't know. They sure liked having my toys in their stores."

Carly resisted an urge to pat Jonah sympathetically on the thigh. She felt a greater urge to shake Sylvia silly. It sounded like she'd handled the situation so tactlessly, she'd left Jonah with deep suspicions of every offer of friendship.

"Jonah," Carly said. "Don't give us toys. Don't give us money. This year, why don't you give yourself? Sign up for the Christmas Tree Roundup, or help cook the dinner. It won't cost you a thing. And, believe me, you'll feel wonderful when Christmas morning comes. The night before Christmas Eve when Mom and I deliver the presents from the Giving Tree—it's more fun than any Christmas morning I can remember as a child."

"You must have had a sad childhood," Jonah said.

"I had a *wonderful* childhood," Carly argued. "But this is better. Try it once, Jonah, and see. I bet you'll love it, too. You can't fool me." She touched his chest. "I know you've got a heart in here, I learned that the night...uh..." Her cheeks flamed and she tried to remove her hand. But she didn't move quickly enough.

Jonah covered her hand with his, pressing it to his chest. "Okay, it's a bet."

His palm on hers reminded her too intensely of the night when his hand had done all those wonderful things to her body. "A bet?" Her voice came out croaky.

He met her eyes, his sparkling with meaning. "You know what you're wagering if you lose?"

Carly felt like she was melting into the chair. She opened her mouth and shut it again. "Lose?"

"Yeah," Jonah said. "Let's define it. I'll be honest. If I enjoy this Christmas as much as you say, you win, and I'll bring toys for every kid who wants one. If I don't, you lose. And I get—"

Carly tugged her hand free. "I know what you get."

Jonah's grin broadened, traveling to his eyes. "Actually that *would* make it my favorite Christmas."

"Oh, shush!" Carly exclaimed quietly, sure everyone left at the party was staring at them. "Is that all you—"

"Hell, no," Jonah said. "But it's hard to forget, you have to admit."

"I do *not* admit it, Jonah," Carly said. "Actually I've put it from my mind."

Jonah stared at her a moment, disbelief clear in his frown. Then he threw back his head and laughed heartily. "You may be able to fool yourself, Silk, but you can't fool me. Maybe this bet is just what *you* need."

"I can't imagine what you're talking about." Carly's voice was getting stiffer and stiffer.

"A few hours in each other's company, unable to touch each other—" Jonah ran his palm softly along her forearm, grinning when she couldn't suppress a quiver "—and maybe you'll admit you've got needs, too." He shook his head. "It'll be an unnatural situation, though. We'll both be frustrated as hell. Are you sure you want to bet?"

When Jonah touched her—with his hands and sometimes even with just his voice—Carly did feel an ache of frustration so intense it surprised her. But it didn't worry her. Despite what Jonah seemed to believe, it wasn't a need, it was simply a desire. She could easily rise above such feelings. Hadn't she done so for years?

Jonah's cynicism and mistrust of people was a more important issue. She knew how much she loved delivering presents every year dressed in her elf suit. She thought about Jonah's instinctive kindness toward her the night she was lonely. His behavior then seemed in such conflict with the Scrooge he became when he talked about business.

Poor thing, she thought. He was the classic case of someone who needed to relearn his faith in his fellow man.

"I'll bet," Carly said. "But you have to really give, you can't be halfhearted."

Jonah nodded. "I don't feel halfhearted about anything with you, Silk. Trust me." His voice softened. "Or maybe I mean, try me." He leaned his head closer.

Next morning as she cleaned up the shop after the party, Carly could still feel his suggestive voice slithering down her spine, his warm breath on the side of her throat. If someone hadn't called her away that moment, she hated to think what might have happened—right there in the middle of the party.

After gathering together all the sign-up sheets, Carly saw Jonah's large bold signature on every page. He'd volunteered for both tree gathering days, both tree delivering days, and one day of decorating the trees for people who couldn't manage to decorate their own; he offered to help cook the Christmas dinner, to help index the Giving Tree cards, and to deliver the presents when they were collected.

Whether or not Carly thought it was a good idea, between now and Christmas, she and Jonah were going to spend every weekend together, and several weekdays. Not just together: together doing things Carly loved.

For just a moment, she wished fervently that she could

look forward to those days. She wanted so much to see if he would enjoy helping people at Christmas.

Instead she'd have to spend the time walking a fine line between enjoying Jonah's company and keeping him at arm's length. And she knew she'd get no help from Jonah in the arm's length department. He'd made it abundantly clear that he'd bet simply to spend time with Carly.

The idea gave her shudders. She told herself she was shuddering in nervousness, but her heart knew she was shuddering with pleasurable anticipation.

The following Saturday, at 6:00 a.m., Carly stood in the parking lot by the city baseball diamond, dressed in warm outdoor clothing, watching snow fall from the dark sky while she waited for the other tree gatherers to arrive. She shivered, wondering how many would back out after they checked the weather.

This was Carly's favorite kind of day: a snowstorm with enough wind to make it dramatic, and cold. But her favorite pastime on such days was building a big fire in the woodstove, making cocoa and reading a book.

A pickup truck drove toward her. Snow swirled in the tunnel of its headlights, and she had no idea who it was. But the engine sounded large. When the driver cut the motor and shut off his lights, the darkness and silence seemed total.

"Morning," Jonah's voice came through the gloom. "Are we the only two who made it?"

"So far," Carly said. "But I'm sure the others will be here soon. At least some of them."

"Why aren't you waiting in your car instead of in this snow?" he asked.

"Mom dropped me off."

Jonah opened the door of his truck. "Let's wait inside."

She walked toward the pickup, getting a closer look at it. "Are you planning to take this into the forest? It looks brand new."

"It's not," Jonah said. "We just keep it cleaned up because we use it for business."

In the dim light, Carly noticed the Jonah's Toys logo painted on the door in bright crayon colors. She wondered what Sylvia thought of donating her truck to Wide Spot's Christmas. But maybe she didn't know.

She climbed in and slid across the seat. Jonah followed. On the dash, he had mittens, a hat, and a large green thermos.

"Coffee?" he offered.

"I think I'll pass for now," Carly said. "We'll be in the forest all day, and it's cold, and the less coffee I have to worry about, the better."

Jonah grinned. "How many other women come along on this?"

"A few," Carly said. "Mostly men come today. The women prefer tomorrow when we deliver the trees."

"Ah," Jonah grinned. "Striking another blow for feminism."

"Well, we don't see many men doing the decorating for the older people who can't do their own, either."

"You do all of it, though, right?" Jonah said.

"Yes, I do," Carly answered, feeling defensive at his tone. "I like it, Jonah. It's what I do for Christmas. Don't you like Christmas at all?"

"Yeah, I like it," Jonah said. "Of course we're busy as hell in the business. But I reach a point when I get to kick back and enjoy my own Christmas. When do you do that?"

"I make a big Christmas breakfast for Mom and me," Carly said. "But we agreed not to buy each other things till—"

"I don't think DeeDee agreed, Silk."

"I beg your pardon," Carly said, annoyed. "Are you telling me what my own mother thinks?"

"Yeah, I am," Jonah said. "I talked to her the other night. She agrees with me, you do too much for everyone else and nothing for yourself. *She* thinks you two ought to get each other presents at Christmas, but she says you refuse every year."

"That's right," Carly said. "And I'm going to go on refusing until I don't owe anybody anything. *Then* I'll think about what presents I want for Christmas."

"You don't owe anybody anything *now*," Jonah said. "Your father's debts died with him."

"You're wrong," Carly said bitterly. "My father's debts haunted us. The estate had to sell *everything*. And even that didn't come close to paying them off."

"DeeDee told me that," Jonah said. "But what didn't get paid, Silk, *isn't* your responsibility. You're being noble past the point of good sense."

Carly clutched the door handle on her side. "Jonah, my father gave me a BMW when I was sixteen. I went to private schools, wore expensive clothes, took outrageously expensive vacations, summer and winter. If I didn't pay back the people who financed all that unearned luxury, I'd feel like a thief." She opened the door. "I don't expect you to understand that. Just don't belittle it." She pulled her stocking hat back on and jumped out into the snow. "I'll just check and see if anyone's coming."

"Carly!" Jonah said as she slammed the door.

He opened his door and came around the truck after

her. She couldn't run away from him, they were going to be tree hunting together all day.

Besides, now that she was outside in the cold, she thought maybe she had overreacted. No doubt it was because she'd already had this discussion too often with DeeDee. But she also seemed jumpier these days, more emotional. Ever since she met Jonah, the tiniest little thing seemed to set her off.

Jonah stood in front of her and put his hands on the hood of the truck behind her. His body sheltered her from the snow.

"I don't want to talk about all that today, Jonah," she said. "This is my Christmas. Whatever you think of it, please let me enjoy it."

Jonah made a motion of zipping his lips. "Not another word, Silk." He looked up as another truck turned off the street into the parking lot. "Looks like we'll get at least one other helper."

"Thank God," Carly muttered, more thankful that she wouldn't be alone with Jonah all day than that they would have help cutting and hauling trees.

Jonah grinned at her. Even in the dim light, she could see he knew exactly what she meant. He pulled on a fleece ski cap and went to meet the new arrival.

An hour later, Carly unclenched her fingers from the seat cushion, opened the passenger door, and jumped out of the truck. "You grew up on a ranch, didn't you?" she said to Jonah as the other pair of tree hunters, Mac and his son, Greg, climbed out of the backseat of the cab.

Jonah pulled on his cap as he came around the truck. "Yeah, how'd you know?"

"Only ranchers drive these back roads as though they're the highway."

They'd driven up to this high bench on a narrow rutted dirt track that wound sharply up the sides of the hills. The land they drove through belonged to a rancher who donated twenty trees every year to the Christmas Tree Roundup. The rest of the volunteers were tree hunting in the national forest, driving on Forest Service maintained gravel roads. At the moment, Carly envied them.

Mac, also a rancher, slapped Jonah on the back. "Thought you drove fine, son. Last year took us half the day to get up here."

Carly gritted her teeth, wishing again she could have gone in one of the other trucks. But Jonah had made it crystal clear with nothing more than a thunderous look that if Carly didn't join the group in his truck, he'd be heading back to Bozeman before another snowflake fell.

"Which do you want, Carly?" Jonah asked. "The chain saw or the handsaw?"

"Are you kiddin'?" Mac said, grabbing the huge chain saw. "We only bring that darn handsaw for Carly." He gestured vaguely toward the tree line. "We'll take the east end. C'mon, Greg."

Carly squinted through the falling snow at the thick tree cover not far ahead of them. "Maybe Greg would like to—"

"Don't even think about it, Carly," Jonah cut her off.

Carly glared at him, irritated that he meant to control her whole Christmas experience. She reached into the back of the truck for the saw. "I like meeting new people at Christmas, Jonah. Maybe we should all go together."

"The hell," he said.

He strapped the handsaw to a small backpack containing his thermos, a water bottle and a couple of sandwiches, then gestured for Carly to lead the way. After a few slips, she found her footing in the snow and moved ahead at a reasonable pace.

"You can drive home if you want, Silk," he said behind her. "You could have asked me to slow down, you know."

"I didn't really think you were driving dangerously," she said. "Just faster than I wanted to go."

"And why," he went on in a tone of exaggerated patience, "does everyone else get a chain saw and we get this antiquated device?"

Carly was glad to be in the lead where Jonah couldn't see the pink in her cheeks. "I, uh, hate the noise and the smell of those things. It just destroys the whole Christmassy feel of the day." She turned, holding her hands out to catch falling flakes. "Listen to the quiet, Jonah. Isn't it beautiful? Doesn't it feel like we've stepped backward into the last century?"

"Oh, absolutely." Jonah's tone held a hint of teasing irony, but his smile was full and genuine. "Too bad we don't have a sled instead of that crummy big-cab, well-heated, four-wheel-drive pickup."

"A sled," Carly rhapsodized, turning up her head to catch a snowflake on her tongue. "Oh, Jonah, that would be perfect. Just perfect." Flakes fell on her cheeks and she turned in a circle, stumbling and nearly toppling into Jonah.

He caught her waist and held her. "A sled would be *almost* perfect, Silk. We'd also need a big pile of furs on the sled, and two fewer people up here in the woods with us."

Carly spun away from him. She pressed cold mittens to her flaming face. "I—I'm sorry. I shouldn't have started that. I…don't…" She shook her head. "I should have gone with Mac."

Jonah gave her shoulders a quick reassuring squeeze from behind. "Nah, Mac uses a chain saw. You'd hate it."

"I would," she breathed. "But we can't—"

"I know," Jonah said. "I told you this would drive me nuts. Do you know how adorable you look with snow falling on your face? Too bad it's *not* a hundred years ago—your reputation would already be ruined just coming up here alone with me. So we could forget convention and—"

"Jonah!"

He held up his hands in surrender. "Let's cut some trees." He pulled his cap off for a second and dragged his hand through his hair as he made that growling noise she'd come to learn was a sign of deep frustration. "I'll lead so I don't have to watch your cute little tush wiggling ahead of me up the trail." He strode past her.

At first Jonah's irritation came as a relief to Carly. In fact, it made their proximity easier. But when he didn't say a word, even when she pointed out the perfect little tree to him, remorse began to hit her. She didn't want all his memories of the day to be bad ones.

"This one?" he said.

Carly nodded. "Yes, don't you think it's just perfect?"

"We've already discussed perfect. Better not start it again." Jonah leaned down and began sawing the base of the tree.

Carly blushed at his innuendo and his rebuke. She certainly didn't want to tease him. She vowed silently to call Sylvia first thing Monday morning to see if they were ready for another mediation session. She couldn't spend much more time with Jonah this way.

"You don't have to cut them all," she said. "If you saw this one, I'll—"

"I'll cut the trees," he said. "We'll get done faster."

Carly sighed and plopped down on the snow. After one catch, Jonah's arm moved back and forth in perfect rhythm. He was right, she never sawed that smoothly. Still, she'd cut plenty of trees on these tree gathering days.

"Are you in such a rush?"

Jonah stopped and looked at her stretched out in the snow. "Not really, I guess. It's frustrating but—" he looked around the forest "—it is beautiful. And the company's as good as it gets." He met her gaze, his lids lowering slightly. "But it does remind me of…other times we spent together."

Carly reached for the hem of her stocking cap and pulled it over her eyes.

Jonah laughed. "Are you an ostrich? You'd do better to cover your luscious mouth that keeps getting you into such messes."

"Go back to cutting," Carly said, raising her cap. "I'll choose the conversational tangents."

"I can hardly wait," he said, his arm moving again in rhythm.

"Tell me about your life on the ranch," Carly said, glad he'd gotten over his annoyance. "How many sisters *do* you have? Any brothers?"

Jonah hesitated a moment, then spoke without looking up from the tree. "There were seven of us."

"Seven!" Carly sat up straight. "I always wanted a larger family. But seven—that's huge!"

Jonah just grunted.

Carly frowned at him though he kept his eyes on the saw. "I didn't mean to offend you, Jonah. It just seems like a lot of kids to try to raise and put through school in today's economy.''

"You're right about that," Jonah said noncommittally.

Carly wished she could see his face, read the emotion in his expressive eyes. "Why do I get the feeling that this topic makes you uncomfortable? Or are you still mad about...something else?"

Jonah stood with the small tree in his fist. "I'm not mad." He looked at the tree. "Shall we just leave the trees where we cut them and pick them up on the way back?" A gleam came into his eyes. "Or shall we dust them first?"

"Dust?" Carly asked suspiciously. Leaping up, she began backing away from the wicked look in his eyes.

Jonah grabbed the tree with both hands, lifted it over her head and shook. Icy snow cascaded all over her.

"Jonah, quit!" Carly shrieked as she ran up the hill laughing.

Jonah dropped the tree and started after her. "I knew I could get you to move a little faster."

Carly brushed snow off her shoulders and took off her hat to shake it out. "Honestly, Jonah." She tried to sound disapproving but she couldn't help returning his grin. "If you don't want to talk about something, just say so. You don't have to drown me to get me to shut up."

Jonah shrugged, not looking repentant. "Sorry, I couldn't resist." His grin faded. "I wasn't trying to get you to shut up. I just...don't talk about that stuff very often. Uh, ever."

"About the size of your family?" Carly asked. "Or are we talking about something more personal?"

"The four youngest kids, a brother and three sisters, were really my cousins," Jonah said.

An undertone in his voice made Carly's heart catch. She didn't know what he was going to tell her but she sensed it was something that hurt deeply.

"They came to stay with us when my mom and my aunt, they were sisters, went on a trip together to Seattle. They were...uh, killed in a fast-food restaurant by a vicious murdering bastard who came into the place and just started mowing people down with an automatic rifle." His hand clenched into a fist so tight it strained the seams of his mitts. "He had no motive. He wasn't a disgruntled employee or anything. He was just insane."

"Oh, no." Carly stopped in her tracks, finding it hard to breathe. "Oh, dear God. How...what..."

Jonah stepped up beside her and brought her back into his arms, undemandingly. She didn't fight him this time, she couldn't.

"Oh, Jonah," she said into his parka. "How awful. No wonder you can't put violence into anything you do."

He hugged her hard against his chest. "I'm glad you understand that."

"How could anyone not understand that?" Carly said. "Dear heaven, what you must have gone through! How old were you?"

"Ten."

"So young."

"Yeah, but I was the oldest," he said. "There were six other kids without mothers, younger than me. The youngest wasn't even one." He rubbed one hand absently up and down her back. "My aunt's husband was a no-good. No one even knew where he was. Dad never thought twice about raising all the kids."

"He must be a wonderful man," Carly said. "How did he manage and still run a ranch?"

Jonah gave a bark of a laugh. "Oh, he had help in the house. Me."

"You?" Carly drew back to look at him. "What about your sisters?"

"The next oldest was Tory, she was nine," Jonah said. "But she'd been a dyed-in-the-wool rancher since she was three years old. She didn't change. The others were too little. So I kind of became...the mom."

"The mom?" Carly felt her lips pulling into a smile. "*That's* why you have such a thing about children."

"Not exactly," Jonah said. "I always liked kids, the way Tory always liked ranching. That's why I didn't mind taking care of them. At least at first."

"Only at first?"

"I'm not a saint," Jonah said. "Kids can be a pain, even ones you love. And I did turn into a teenage boy, with a different agenda. Lots of times I'd complain that I never got to do stuff with my friends. Then I'd tell Tory I wanted to do the ranching and she could stay with the kids."

Carly tried to imagine this big muscular man as a teenager with dishpan hands but the picture wouldn't form. He was too masculine. Then she pictured him with a baby in his hands and she had to shut her eyes against the warm rush of feelings.

"So did she trade with you when you asked?"

"In a way," Jonah said, a hint of bitterness in his voice. "She'd wait till it was about thirty below, then tell me I could feed the cows that day. Naturally I'd give up the whole idea damn quick. Besides, when I'd get inside after feeding, Tory would have the breakfast burned and all the kids crying because they didn't have the right clothes on or something. She was a disaster in the house. And I...well, I didn't want the little kids to be unhappy.''

Carly was smiling so hard her eyes teared. ''How many mornings like that did it take to convince you that you didn't want to switch jobs?''

Jonah's lips twitched but he fought the smile. ''Not too many. I'm not stupid. I'm sure Tory chose those cold mornings on purpose, she's not stupid, either.''

Carly couldn't tell if Jonah carried a resentment toward his sister. ''Was she usually that sneaky when she wanted something?''

''Well, she...'' Jonah frowned, and it grew deeper and seemed to turn inward. ''No, actually. She never could lie. Got herself into trouble more than once because she was so damn honest.'' The frown was melting. ''I used to tell her to practice in front of a mirror, but she could never pull off a believable lie.''

''I'd like to meet her,'' Carly said. ''To see you two together.''

A grim look flashed over Jonah's face. ''Tory and I...we're not as close as we used to be.''

''Don't you see her, and the rest of your family, at Christmas?''

''I send presents.'' His flat tone made it clear that he was through discussing his family.

It also shattered the mood. Carly shut her eyes, remembering all at once that she was mediating a dispute between Jonah and his business partner and sometime lover. With alacrity, she disentangled herself from his arms.

''We'd better get going,'' she said, ''or we'll never get our ten trees before dark.''

Jonah reached across the chilly space between them

and lifted her chin on the edge of his snowy mitt. She let her gaze meet his. "I haven't told anyone that stuff for years, Carly. It always hurt so much to talk about it that I never wanted to. It's different with you, kind of…cathartic."

"I'm glad, Jonah. I didn't mean to pry."

"I'll tell you when you're prying." He dropped his hand. "We click, Silk. How much longer do you think you can pretend you're just my mediator?"

Carly's lips trembled but her voice was steady. "Till we're done…which will probably seem like…"

"Years?"

"Millennia."

Jonah released her. "You got that right." He started up the hill.

CHAPTER FIVE

CARLY looked with relief at the last tree in the back of Jonah's pickup. Spending a second day alone with him, while carefully avoiding a repeat of yesterday's closeness, had kept her stomach knotted up so tight all day she felt almost queasy. She craved solitude and a long, hot bubble bath.

This morning, Carly had started her strategy of keeping distance between them when she made up the lists of who would deliver which trees. She had put all the organizations—churches, the businesses, the grade school, the day care—on her and Jonah's list.

As the day progressed, Carly began to feel a little guilty. After all, she'd talked Jonah into this by telling him how good he'd feel helping others, especially kids. It was hard to get a lot of good feeling from dropping a tree on the front porch at the day care.

But a town the size of Wide Spot didn't have all that many organizations in need of trees. By noon, Carly had scratched all those names off their list, and they had no one left but families.

Phase Two of her Don't Get Close To Jonah Plan had been to put so many names on their list that they couldn't stop too long at any one house for the coffee and cookies they were always offered. That way, Carly wouldn't relax and enjoy Jonah's company.

He obviously knew exactly what she was doing. His sardonic grin grew broader after each rushed visit.

And it didn't work anyway. Not even close. Carly's

heart had begun to melt toward him at the very first house. The four-year-old twin boys, whose father had been killed six months ago in a mine accident, had politely thanked Jonah for the tree. But he had overheard them whispering to each other that it wasn't as big as the one they cut last year with Daddy.

Over their mother's embarrassed protests, Jonah scooped up the twins and carried them out to his truck to choose their own tree. Patiently he held up each of the remaining trees, propping the boys' favorites against the side of the truck for further inspection. When they finally settled on the tallest, broadest one, Jonah let them carry it inside themselves, with only a little unobvious help from him, as if they'd chopped it down on their own.

Watching from inside, Carly listened to the boys' mother praise Jonah's kindness and humor. She couldn't disagree with a word the woman said. But, despite the tears stinging her eyes, she couldn't let herself enjoy it, either.

At house after house, Jonah seemed to positively revel in giving pleasure to the children. Carly wondered why it came as such a surprise to her. The man made toys for children for heaven's sake! Of course he must care about what they liked.

With a sigh of relief that the emotionally taxing day was nearly over, Carly reached into the back of the truck and pulled out the last tree.

"Maybe I should take this one inside myself, Jonah," she said, looking up the walk to the front door of the house. "Mrs. Watson said she didn't want a tree this year."

Jonah raised a brow. "And you got her one anyway?"

"I did because..." Carly chewed her bottom lip.

"Well, everyone needs a Christmas. And she's all alone and..."

Jonah took the tree. "You're either a do-gooder or a meddler, Silk. I haven't decided which one yet." He started up the walk, speaking over his shoulder. "Maybe having a tree will just remind her how alone she is. Did you ever think of that?"

"Well, yes, but I thought maybe if she had the tree, she'd come to the community dinner, and maybe even let someone take her to church on Christmas." Carly expelled a sigh. "I know it's meddling. But if she did those things, she wouldn't be quite so alone and lonely."

Jonah stopped at the foot of the steps and turned to her. "Doesn't she have any family around here? What about her friends?"

"She has one daughter, who lives back east. And she *does* have friends," Carly said. "She just doesn't believe it."

Jonah raised a brow. "What is she—the old crone of the town or something? Always been a terror, has she?"

"Oh, no," Carly said. "She was very happy until about eight years ago, when her husband and best friend died the same year."

Jonah still looked dubious. "She only had one friend?"

"She seems to think so," Carly said sadly. "The next year she found out she has Parkinson's disease, and she quit going out much. She's embarrassed that she can't walk well, or talk as clearly as she used to. If she saw people more..."

Jonah rolled his eyes. "That settles one thing, Ms. Underbrook."

"What's that?" Carly said.

"In this case, you're definitely meddling." He put a

fist on his hip and gave her a demanding look. "Aren't you?"

"Uh…" Carly examined the tree as if it was the most fascinating thing she'd ever seen.

"The tree is just the first step in a major plot, isn't it?" Jonah didn't sound all that disapproving, so Carly brought her gaze up to his. The black-brown eyes regarded her with amusement.

Carly made a face at him. "I see her every day, you know. I deliver meals-on-wheels. Most of the people who need them come to town hall every day and eat with others. They enjoy the company. Mrs. Watson would, too."

Jonah shook his head in mock dismay. At least she thought it was mock. He *was* smiling. "I hope you never take me on as one of your cases, Silk. You interfere in such a determined way."

Carly gave him a little grin. "And why do you think you're helping me deliver trees, Jonah?" She shook a finger at him. "You'll be happier soon, too, just wait and see."

Jonah's dark brows rose. "You, too, Ms. Underbrook, when you admit you are just as needy as Mrs. Watson. Then it will be my singular pleasure to make *you* happier."

"I do have needs, Jonah—I need to be independent."

"Sure." Jonah nodded. "Ask yourself tonight, when you're alone in your bed, why you really made this bet with me. Couldn't be that you just wanted to spend time with me, could it?"

Carly opened her mouth to deny it, but the thought that he might be right dried up her words. "I'm calling Sylvia tomorrow to set up your next appointment," she was surprised to hear herself say.

Jonah laughed. "Good idea." He picked up the tree. "C'mon. Let's get this over with so the poor woman can go back to her pleasant solitary life."

Knowing that it was too hard for Mrs. Watson to get to the door, Carly knocked but didn't wait for a response.

"Mrs. Watson?" she called as she opened the door. "We've brought you a lovely little Christmas tree."

"That you, Carly?" Mrs. Watson's quavery voice came from the living room. "I told you I didn't want a tree this year. Don't you even bring it in here."

Carly held the door open and gestured for Jonah to take the tree inside. He rolled his eyes but did as she said.

"Hi, Mrs. Watson," Carly said cheerfully as she led Jonah toward the front room. "I want you to meet a friend of mine, Jonah St. John. He's helping with the trees this year, and as soon as we saw this one we knew it would be perfect for you."

"Speak for yourself," Jonah muttered under his breath, then, "How do you do, Mrs. Watson?"

"I don't want it." Mrs. Watson grabbed her cane, which was resting against her chair, and pounded the floor for emphasis. "Take that right out of here, young man."

"Mrs. Watson," Jonah said. "I know how you feel. I've been standing on your walk arguing with her for thirty minutes. But she's a very determined woman."

"So am I." Mrs. Watson's voice was growing stronger the more she talked. With the help of her walker, she pulled herself to her feet. "I'm not entirely helpless, you know. If you leave that infernal bush here, I'll find a way to throw it out."

"Oh, Mrs. Watson," Carly said. "Don't do that." She stepped closer to give the older woman's shoulders a quick squeeze. "If it really makes you unhappy, we'll take it away. But you know how a pretty tree can light up your spirits as well as the room. We'll put it up for you, we'll decorate it, we'll take it down after Christmas, we'll even sweep up all the needles. All you have to do is enjoy looking at it."

"Enjoy!" Mrs. Watson snapped. "Just reminds me Cyrus is dead, my daughter never calls me and my ungrateful grandchildren never thank me for their gifts."

Mrs. Watson's left leg, the weaker one, began to tremble. Jonah dropped the tree to catch her by the arm.

"Let me give you a hand, Mrs. Watson."

"I don't need your help, young man," Mrs. Watson snapped. "What do you think I do around here alone all day? Call for help every time my leg bothers me?"

"Of course not," Jonah said. "I don't think you're helpless. But it'd make me feel useful if you'd let me make things a little easier for you during the few minutes we're visiting." He gave her the kind of smile that would have dissolved Carly's resistance. "Please?"

Mrs. Watson smiled, a broader smile than Carly was used to seeing on the old woman's face. But she directed it at Carly, not Jonah. "You'd better watch out for this one, Carly, or you will find yourself in trouble."

"Believe me, Mrs. Watson, I already know that."

Gently, Jonah helped her back into her chair. Mrs. Watson didn't even give him the resentful look she always gave Carly when she thought Carly was being overly solicitous. In fact the woman was practically simpering.

Once again, Carly felt her eyelids burn with unshed tears. But this time they were tears of sadness. If this lonely old woman could be melted so fast by Jonah, she needed more than a donated Christmas tree to fill the gaps in her solitary life.

Jonah must recognize that, too. He sat on the arm of her chair and took her hand. "I can understand why you're annoyed with your family. Families can be... difficult. But this tree doesn't come from them. It comes from your friends, right here in Wide Spot. You must believe Carly's your friend, don't you?"

"Of course I do," Mrs. Watson said. She cast Carly a quick look of approval.

"Well, if you know that much about her, you must have figured out that if you don't take this tree, she'll just do something else to make you feel Christmassy. And she'll probably drag me into that one, too." He gave a long-suffering sigh. "You'd really help me out if you'd just let her put up the darn tree and pretend you like it."

"Oh, for pity's sake," Mrs. Watson said, freeing her hand. "All right, I'll take the tree. Are you going to put it up right now? I was about to take a nap."

"We'll just put it in water today," Carly said happily. "We'll be back to decorate it Thursday afternoon."

"We will?" Jonah asked.

"Certainly," Carly said meaningfully. "You volunteered, remember? In writing."

Jonah looked like he wanted to strangle her but he kept his mouth shut.

"There's caroling after," she went on, ignoring their sour looks, "if you want. Then cocoa and—"

"Carly Underbrook," Mrs. Watson said, "if you think for one second you can trick me into singing because you bring a handsome man over to decorate my Christmas tree, well you can just think again." She pursed her lips in irritation. "You come Wednesday to decorate my tree or don't bother to come at all."

Jonah was looking back and forth between Carly and Mrs. Watson, suspicion growing in his eyes. "Tried this before, has she?" he asked the older woman.

"Annually." Mrs. Watson picked up her cane to shake it at Carly. "And it won't work any better this year than it ever did before. I can't sing anymore, Carly, and you know it."

"I don't know any such thing," Carly said. "Maizey says you still have a better voice than anyone in town."

"Oh, what does she know?" Mrs. Watson snapped. "Plays the organ so loud, she probably can't hear any of us."

"Everyone can hear you," Carly insisted. She turned to Jonah. "Mrs. Watson used to sing with the Metropolitan Opera in New York."

"Really?" Jonah asked her.

"Many years ago," Mrs. Watson said. "When my voice didn't sound like a leaf trembling in the wind." She grabbed her walker and rattled it as if to show how her voice trembled. "So just forget it, Carly Underbrook."

"But you—"

"Hold it." Jonah pushed a palm toward Carly. "Irresistible force meet immovable object." He muttered, standing. "C'mon, Silk, let's get the tree in water. You two can continue this battle later." He grinned down at Mrs. Watson. "By the time you're a hundred, you'll know every move by heart."

"A hundred," Mrs. Watson sniffed. "Look out for him, Carly. Don't say I didn't warn you."

Tuesday morning, Carly paced around her tiny mediator's office, wishing the meeting with Sylvia were already over. When she'd made the appointment the day before, she had been relieved at the idea of getting herself and Jonah out of this awkward and peculiar relationship.

But this morning, for some reason, she woke with her stomach knotted at the thought of the meeting. Even the smell of DeeDee's bacon made her queasy, and she'd come downstairs to breakfast on *biscotti* from the gift shop.

No doubt it was her nagging guilt over her entangled situation with Sylvia and Jonah. She should never have gotten into this mediation, she shouldn't have held back from Sylvia about her relationship with Jonah. But Carly hadn't really had a relationship with Jonah. And she certainly hadn't planned to pursue one.

But she couldn't lie to herself—her behavior with him on the Christmas tree days hadn't been entirely.... Carly let that thought trickle off, not wanting to characterize her actions on those days, even to herself. Or rather *especially* to herself. Her mind might dredge up feelings she didn't want to acknowledge at all.

When Jonah and Sylvia arrived, Carly was just opening her second package of *biscotti*. Away from the smell of frying bacon, her appetite had reasserted itself. She put the biscuits on the table with cream and sugar and poured coffee for all of them.

"We picked a beautiful morning for this meeting," Carly began, hoping to get an idea of their moods before she opened any serious discussion. "I hope you enjoyed the drive over."

"Mmmph." Jonah barely nodded.

Carly wondered at his unresponsiveness. Perhaps he dreaded the coming confrontation as much as she did.

"It's pretty enough," Sylvia said, "but I have another meeting in West Yellowstone in a few hours. Can we get right down to business?"

"Of course," Carly said. "Let's begin with you, Sylvia. In your talks with Jonah since our last meeting, do you feel you have made any progress?"

"Not an iota," Sylvia snapped. "I'm nearly ready to see a lawyer." She made a quick gesture with her hand. "Oh, not as a mediator, but to start a lawsuit. Jonah won't budge, neither will I." She glared at her partner. "I'm sure a judge will agree that, no matter who holds the patents to these toys, the remaining company—which I'm sure will be *me*—could continue to sell any toys created before the business broke up." She sounded unyielding, as if any desire she'd once had to work things out had vanished.

Carly stared, trying to make her jaw muscles behave and keep her mouth from flopping open. She hadn't meant for Sylvia to go so far so quickly. She had simply wanted to know if they had resolved their problems together. If Sylvia had said yes, Carly wouldn't have to go into all the reasons she felt obligated to disqualify herself as mediator.

Carly should never have let Sylvia begin, but now that she had, she wasn't sure what step to take next. "Ah…" She paused. "Sylvia, I'm not sure that—"

Sylvia made that sharp throwaway gesture again. "Ask Jonah how he feels about a lawsuit. Remind him if he isn't more reasonable, that'll be his only other choice. And remember, Jonah, if a judge decides that I get the company, I'll be able to sell whatever kinds of toys I want under the Jonah's Toys name."

A muscle twitched in Jonah's jaw. "Shall I answer?"

he asked Carly. "Or do you want to try to Milquetoast up Sylvia's remarks?"

Carly covered her face for a second, then immediately lowered her hands. This was about Sylvia and Jonah, not her. "I don't want you to answer at all, Jonah." She faced his partner. "Sylvia, I don't like to leave this problem in the middle this way, but I feel I must withdraw as your mediator."

"Withdraw?" Sylvia demanded. "You can't do that *now*, can you? I'm sure it's unethical. You've heard all about our personal problems as well as our business ones. I told you how much I love Jonah, and now you want to *quit*?"

Carly swallowed. "Believe me, I'm not going to talk about anything I've learned here to anyone else. Unless you'd like me to explain my view of the problem to your new mediator. I can't even be called as a witness, if you do go to court. But I don't think I can maintain my neutrality. So I don't believe I can help you."

"Neutrality?" Sylvia swung one foot sharply back and forth. "What would make you stop feeling neutral? We haven't even seen you for two weeks." Her tawny eyes shifted to Jonah then back to Carly. "At least, *I* haven't seen you. But then, I haven't seen much of Jonah, either."

"Exactly," Carly said, relieved to get the whole thing out in the open. "I have seen Jonah. Not privately, of course, but enough that I—"

"Seen Jonah?" Sylvia exclaimed. "What do you mean by that?" She looked at Jonah. "Is that where you've been all weekend?" She returned her furious glare to Carly. "I want to know exactly what's gone on between you two. If you've stepped out of line, I'll sue you so fast, and so publicly, you'll never get another mediation client. And I'll have no other choice but to take Jonah to court, too.''

Jonah pounded his fist on the table. "Nothing's 'gone on,' Sylvia. Not a goddamn thing.''

Sylvia regarded him ironically, her brows arched. "Why, darling. You seem quite adamant about defending Ms. Underbrook's honor. How...telling.''

Carly shot Jonah a look that, thankfully, kept him from responding. "I'm sure you know that Jonah has volunteered his time to help out with some of Wide Spot's Christmas programs. Those are the times, the only times, I've seen him outside the office. We never discussed anything that had come up during mediation. In fact, we mostly discussed only which Christmas tree to cut next.''

"If that's true, then why can't you continue as mediator?'' Sylvia's gaze locked on Carly's.

"Uh...'' Carly crossed her legs, then uncrossed them. Sylvia's accusatory stare made her feel as if she'd committed a crime. "Because...I don't...''

"Just how serious *are* you about him?''

"Serious?'' Carly exclaimed. "That's...ridiculous. We just met.''

Sylvia gave her the sardonic look she'd given Jonah. "Nearly a month ago, Carly. A lot can happen in a month.''

"Well, it hasn't happened to me,'' Carly said, wondering if she were lying. This was the very subject she had refused to broach in her own thoughts. She wasn't going to ponder her feelings toward Jonah, aloud, in front of him and Sylvia. "But I've seen another side of him, one that is quite, uh...'' Her cheeks were on fire. "...Endearing. The way he is with children and old ladies. I have begun to know him on a personal level. I don't know you that way. So I don't think I can fairly continue.''

Sylvia leaned back, but her posture gave no hint of relaxation. Her shoulders remained straight, her hands folded, her ankles crossed. An X ray couldn't see through Carly more thoroughly than Sylvia's unwavering stare.

Finally she shifted her laserlike gaze to Jonah. ''And how do *you* feel about this, Jonah?'' she asked. ''I assume you two discussed it when you decided to gang up on me this way.''

''You're not listening, Sylvia,'' Jonah returned, his tone equally sarcastic. ''Carly and I discussed little more than Christmas trees.''

Carly stepped in, hoping to deflect a major argument. ''We never talked about anything having to do with the mediation.'' She turned to Jonah. ''How *do* you feel about it? Do you think…'' She struggled for words that would express what she meant yet say nothing to Sylvia. ''…You can keep your negotiations with Sylvia separate from…well, from… Do you think I should continue as your mediator?''

''No,'' Jonah said. ''Carly didn't warn me about this, Sylvia. But I have to agree with her. We've gotten into a situation that's awkward. Just like the way you feel about seeing a mediator in Bozeman, I don't want to discuss our problems with someone I know personally.''

''Personally?'' Sylvia demanded, her voice rising. ''What about *our* personal relationship, Jonah? What chance does that have?'' She blinked her eyes as if fluttering away tears. When Jonah appeared unmoved, she looked at Carly. ''So I'm to understand that as soon as you withdraw, you and Jonah plan to continue this 'personal' affair you've begun?''

"It's not an affair, Sylvia!" Jonah growled.

"Yes, darling," Sylvia said in a saccharine sweet voice. "Call it what you want—it's a betrayal."

"Goddamn it, Sylvia—" Jonah began.

Carly pushed a palm toward him. "Jonah, please."

She couldn't help feeling sorry for Sylvia, who obviously felt outnumbered and stabbed in the back. Carly wished she'd met with her alone and explained the whole thing, woman to woman.

"Sylvia, please don't feel threatened by this. It won't affect your negotiations with Jonah at all."

"Hmmph," Sylvia muttered.

"Truly," Carly continued. "Jonah and I have no plans to see each other while you're in mediation. And even if we did, we would never discuss your negotiations."

Instead of looking mollified, Sylvia looked more suspicious than ever. "I can't talk about this with Jonah here. I feel very uncomfortable, not knowing what the relationship is between you two." She folded her hands again, resting them stiffly in her lap. "I want to talk to you alone before I decide what to do about this. I need to understand what's going on, without the person I'm in a dispute with overhearing my every word."

"Oh, that's very reasonable," Carly said, comfortably slipping into her professional role. "Often when negotiations stall, private meetings with the mediator can get things going again. Would you like to caucus with me now, Sylvia? I'm sure Jonah wouldn't mind waiting for you in the gift shop."

"No," Sylvia said, looking at her watch. "I've got that meeting in West Yellowstone. I don't have time." She pulled a small date calendar out of her purse and studied it. "How about next Monday morning?"

"Fine," Carly said.

"And until then, you and Jonah won't…" She waved a hand back and forth between the two of them.

"I'm not sure what you mean," Carly said primly, annoyed that Sylvia would try to control every aspect of Jonah's life. "We have cut trees, delivered them—"

"Oh, don't be so exact," Sylvia said. "You won't pursue a relationship until you and I have had our meeting."

"No, of course not," Carly said. "I didn't mean to do that anyway."

Sylvia stood. "Very well. Come on, Jonah."

Jonah didn't budge. "I think I'll meet with Ms. Underbrook now, Sylvia," he said. "Since you can't. After all, I think my input on this problem should be considered, too."

Sylvia made a small noise of annoyance. "I…"

"You have your own car," Jonah said. "Better get to your meeting. I'll be back in Bozeman in time to take care of that shipment this afternoon."

"Well, I hope so," Sylvia said. "It's very important."

Jonah looked like he might make a sarcastic reply, then he softened. His shoulders lost that stiff look, his frown eased. "I know it is, Sylvia. I haven't forgotten the business. And I'm not staying to undermine you. I just plan to explain my position on this."

He stood and held Sylvia's coat for her. "Call me on your cell phone when you get out of the meeting and let me know what happened."

That seemed to relax Sylvia. She slipped into her coat and opened the door. "You'll be back at the office by then you think?"

"I'm sure of it."

He shut the door behind her and returned to his chair.

Carly had watched this exchange without getting up. She wished he'd gone, too. She didn't want to make her promise to Sylvia a lie.

Jonah stood again and began pacing. "Did something special bring this on, Silk?"

"Please, Jonah," Carly said, "don't call me Silk here. This is a caucus with your mediator. We're here to discuss the termination of our professional relationship."

"Like hell!" Jonah growled. "I'm here to discuss pursuing our personal relationship, which I find a helluva lot more interesting than—"

"Jonah, hush!" Carly said. "We can't pursue anything right now. Not while you're in mediation. And even more especially not before I talk to Sylvia and explain everything."

Jonah put his hands on the back of the chair opposite Carly. His eyes darkened with humor as a broad smile spread across his face. "And just what are you going to explain to her, Ms. Underbrook? How we…met? Now there's a conversation I'd love to hear."

"No." Carly looked away from him, not wanting him to draw her into his enjoyment. Memories of that night never failed to make her smile even at the most inappropriate moments.

"I have to admit, it was very informative listening to you try to tell Sylvia what you found so endearing about me." Jonah chuckled. "The way I am with children and old ladies. What about the way I am with a woman my own age whom I'd like to get to know better?"

Carly picked up a *biscotti*, broke it in two, then put the pieces back on the plate. "Did you want this caucus just to tease me, Jonah? Or did you really have a purpose?"

He pulled his chair out and sat down. "My purpose

was to warn you that if you think you're going to get out of this mess easily, you're nuts. Sylvia's sense of self-preservation is very strong. She won't let you just quit. Or she'll insist that you quit but demand you put yourself in cold storage or move to Fairbanks or something—now that she knows there's something between us."

"There isn't anything between us, Jonah," Carly insisted.

"Then why quit?"

"Because...because we can't..." She shrugged helplessly. "Because I can't be objective anymore. I..."

Jonah reached across the table and took her hand. Warmth flowed up Carly's arm and she knew she ought to draw her hand away. Instead she let herself savor the feeling.

"Because, Silk, you like me too much. Just as I like you. You can't pretend anymore that there's nothing between us, that's why you're quitting."

"I just don't feel right when I'm with you. I feel that I'm...misleading Sylvia." She tugged on her hand and he released it immediately. "It's just not right."

"What's not right is that you won't admit to yourself what's going on between us." Jonah stood up and grabbed his coat.

"Jonah, the main reason you came to a mediator was to stay out of court," Carly said. "I can't be the cause of making Sylvia file a lawsuit."

"Trust me," Jonah said. "That's not going to happen. Sylvia knows how much she'd lose that way."

"You can't be sure," Carly said. "And as a mediator—"

"This mediation crap is just a phony obstacle you're using to hide your real feelings." He stuck his arms into his coat sleeves. "If it hadn't been for that, you'd have found something else to put up a wall between us."

"I can't know what I'd have done if we met another way, Jonah."

"Ha! When was the last time you let yourself want a man the way you wanted me at that party?"

Carly covered her face with her hands. "This isn't right, we can't talk about this now."

Jonah came around to her side of the table. He grabbed her wrists and pulled her hands down. "I'm not your father, Carly. I'm not going to deceive you. I've been straightforward since our first dance. Now it's time for you to do the same."

"I haven't lied to you, either," Carly said, tears stinging at her lids.

"Yeah?" Taking her face gently between his palms, he leaned down, brushing his lips warmly over hers.

Carly hurt inside, she wanted so much to stretch up and meet his kiss. "Jonah!" she gasped, turning away. "We can't."

Jonah straightened, aggravation clear in his expression. "You're lying to both of us—every time you deny your feelings!"

She caught her bottom lip between her teeth. "I'm sorry everything happened this way, I didn't mean it to. But this week, until I see Sylvia, I just can't..."

"Right," Jonah interrupted. "You can't. Because you're scared."

"I'm not afraid of you," Carly insisted. "And even if I am, that's not what this is about. It's ethics. Jonah, it's only a week."

He shook his head. "I wish I believed that." He made an impatient noise. "But I guess I can wait a week for you to find out the mess you're really in."

His words sounded reasonable, but he slammed the door behind him with enough force to rattle the glass in the windows.

Sniffing, Carly dashed tears off her cheek. Finally she checked her tears by eating the rest of the *biscotti*.

CHAPTER SIX

THURSDAY evening, Carly made the caroling truck daw-dle, hoping it wasn't obvious to everyone she was wait-ing for Jonah. After twice getting the men to rearrange the hay bales on the back of the big flatbed truck into a more tiered structure, she couldn't think of anything else to delay them. She gave up. It wasn't as though she really expected him. He hadn't agreed to go caroling, the way he had those other projects.

Carly had seen him just the night before at Mrs. Watson's house. She hadn't expected him there, either. After his angry departure from their mediation session, she figured he wouldn't be in the mood. But when Carly arrived at Mrs. Watson's house, the voice that called for her to come in was Jonah's.

She was even more surprised by the other sound that greeted her as she opened the door: Christmas music. Jonah had brought a cassette player and several tapes. He said they were ones he'd had for years, but when Carly looked through them, she found two that had never been opened. His kindness to her friend made Carly want to hug him. But of course she resisted.

By the time they got to the star on top of the tree, all three of them were singing the Hallelujah Chorus along with the Mormon Tabernacle Choir. Jonah seemed to enjoy himself as much as the women, and Carly had begun to let herself believe he would want to sing to-night, as well.

Of course he *had* told her that he'd only brought the

music as a way to get to see Carly. His reasoning—as he'd explained when he walked her to her car—was pure male logic. Even though Carly had promised Sylvia she'd stay away from him, he knew she'd never try to kick him out of Mrs. Watson's if it meant depriving the old dear of the music she loved.

"Most people, Silk," he'd said, "operate on enlightened self-interest. You should try it—it's refreshingly honest."

Carly plopped down on one of the hay bales as the caroling truck pulled out of the high school parking lot. She had thought...well, hoped...he'd been kidding. But she'd been wrong.

"Aren't you going to sing, Carly?"

She looked up to see Tommy standing over her. "Oh, right. I... Of course, I'm going to sing. That's what we're here for, isn't it?"

"The rest of us thought so," Tommy said. "DeeDee thinks you'd better start us off."

"Maizey's here," Carly said, standing as the truck came to a stop. "She sings better than—"

"Timing's perfect." She heard Jonah's voice.

Looking up, Carly saw that the truck had stopped directly in front of Mrs. Watson's house. Jonah came down the front walk with a protesting Mrs. Watson in his arms.

"Put me down, young man," she snapped. "This is kidnapping. That's a federal offense. I trusted you in my home, and this is the thanks I get."

"Esther!" Maizey cried. "Merry Christmas. Are you coming with us this year? Why this'll be the best caroling we've had in ages."

One of the men jumped down to help Jonah lift Mrs. Watson into the back of the flatbed truck. Jonah had bundled her in blankets and warm clothes. They rearranged the hay bales one more time to make a seat for her that would protect her from the wind.

Mrs. Watson looked like she was still muttering protests, but her voice couldn't be heard over the voices of other carolers welcoming her. A girl not yet into her teens, whom Carly had never met, stood close to Mrs. Watson, not saying anything.

The truck roared to life and drove to the Wide Spot Nursing Home where many of the residents stood outside in coats and hats, ready to sing with the carolers. Others, who couldn't brave the elements, looked out the windows. As the truck slowed to a stop, the carolers instinctively formed a semicircle with Mrs. Watson at its center. But no one began singing.

"Mrs. Watson," Jonah said, his voice carrying over the conversations in the truck. "No one's going to sing until you do. Everyone's embarrassed to start with you here, with your beautiful voice."

"Young man," Mrs. Watson said sternly. "You are worse than Carly. I didn't think it was possible."

Jonah found Carly with his eyes and gave her a tiny bow. "Thank you, Mrs. Watson. There's no one I'd rather be worse than."

Carly laughed happily, feeling more Christmassy than she had in years. "We're not moving until you sing, Mrs. Watson."

Mrs. Watson glared and made no noise.

Finally the young girl leaned down and said quietly, "Mrs. Watson, I'll sing with you."

"What makes you think I want to sing?" Mrs. Watson looked up at the girl. "Do I know you? What's your name?"

"Annie. And I figured, like, you must want to sing some or, like, you wouldn't be here."

"I was brought here under duress, child." Mrs. Watson looked at the group of old people waiting in the wind to sing along with those in the truck. "Look at those poor people freezing. You begin the singing, Annie."

"With you," Annie said.

"C'mon!" shouted a few people in front of the nursing home. "We're cold.... Start singing."

"Oh, very well." Mrs. Watson gave Jonah a fierce look, then transferred it to Carly. "I *told* you to watch out for him." Turning her head, she whispered to the girl.

The two voices, one young and strong, one quavery but lovely, began singing "Oh Come All Ye Faithful." They were immediately joined by others, on the truck and on the ground. The hymn, Carly's favorite, sounded more beautiful to her than it ever had before.

Even singing, she grinned till her eyes teared. Mrs. Watson had glared when she looked at Carly, she'd tried to look like she was furious at being drawn into this. But there was a sparkle of happiness in her faded blue eyes that Carly had never seen before.

Impulsively, Carly turned and hugged Jonah hard. She meant it to be a quick platonic hug. But Jonah returned it with both his arms and nothing about him felt platonic. Without a great deal of movement, he tugged her behind the circle of singers into the shadow of the tallest tier of bales.

"Oh, Jonah," Carly whispered, hoping he could hear her over the carolers. "Thank you. You have a heart of gold." She squirmed a little. "Now please, let's sing."

She squirmed harder. "Jonah, let me go. We're in sight of practically everyone I know."

"They don't see out their backs," Jonah murmured, a devilish glint in his eye that made Carly quiver. "Besides, none of 'em know me. Maybe I should show them what really lures me to Wide Spot." His mouth came closer to hers. "Because it's not singing."

"Jonah, please." Carly's voice came out almost a whimper. She was grateful the singers were loudly in the middle of "God Rest Ye Merry Gentlemen." "We can't do this. I promised Sylvia."

"*Damn*, I'm sick of hearing about Sylvia," Jonah growled, sounding frustrated and angry.

Carly sighed with relief, sure she'd annoyed him enough that he'd let her go. When her guard was down, Jonah covered her mouth with his. Placing one gloved hand at the back of her head, he held her to him.

Carly's sensible mind had less than a second to tell her that such behavior was insane. Then sensation and longing landed a knockout blow to rational thought. She couldn't refuse what Jonah offered. She wanted it too much. His lips massaged hers open, his tongue met hers with motions that drew hers deep into his mouth.

Carly remembered at once that he kissed this way, this special, inviting, incredibly delicious way. She remembered, no matter how much she had lectured herself the past several weeks, because she had never for one instant forgotten. She had kept all those feelings she and Jonah shared in a special place in her heart where she could look at them and call them back every day.

As Jonah's other hand covered her buttocks, Carly realized that intense as her memories were of the emotions, the other feelings felt as new as if this were the first time he'd touched her. The reality of the sensations was far too powerful for mere imagination to bring it to life.

The singing quieted as Mrs. Watson and Annie began the third verse, which no one else seemed to know. The resulting hush brought Carly back to awareness of her surroundings. A torrent of embarrassment washed over her, dousing her desire as effectively as a face-plant in a snowdrift. She twisted free of Jonah's embrace.

Carly looked at the others on the truck. All of them still faced the nursing home. No one seemed to be paying the slightest bit of attention to her and Jonah. Except DeeDee, of course, whose lack of attention seemed so studied Carly didn't believe it for an instant.

Mrs. Watson and Annie got to the chorus, and all the other voices joined in again. Shaky still, especially in the knees, Carly sang, too. She clung to the hay bales for support and refused even to look at Jonah.

What on earth was she going to do next Monday? How could she look Sylvia in the eye when she had been...consorting with Jonah in front of half the town a few nights before? Carly cringed at the thought of pretending that her interest in Jonah was purely professional.

Professional, that was a laugh. Carly could think of a lot of words to describe the kiss they'd just shared, but "professional" wasn't one of them. Obviously, no thought of her career penetrated the luscious sensual haze Jonah's touch created in her.

Jonah stepped closer and lowered his voice. "I'd like to say I'm sorry, Carly. But I can't. I enjoyed that too much." He squeezed her shoulder quickly and released her. "I think we have something special and we're just wasting time. Silk, I just want to forget this mediation drivel and kiss you again. And again. Till you—"

"Jonah!" she whispered fiercely. "You're tormenting me. Can't you see that? I'm not asking you to wait until middle age. Next Monday...a few days."

Jonah shook his head. "You don't know Sylvia. She knows how often I've been over here recently. If she decides that what's going on between us threatens her, she'll keep this negotiation going on forever. Mark my words."

"I won't let her, Jonah," Carly said confidently. "Trust me to know my job."

Jonah nodded, his expression a mix of resignation and skepticism. "You know your job, Silk, but you don't know my partner. You're going to have to be damned determined about throwing in the towel, no matter what her threats. Or let her run your life."

"Jonah, Sylvia's threatening more than me," Carly whispered fiercely. "If I mess this up, she'll take you to court, too. You could lose your business."

Jonah shook his head. "Don't worry about my business, Silk."

Carly bit her lip, stung by his attitude. "You came to me to mediate a problem with your business."

Jonah frowned. "I came because I wanted someone objective to make Sylvia see some sense." He shook his head. "I've already got one woman trying to control my business for me, Silk, I don't need another. Worry about her, not me."

"You're so cynical."

"Yeah? Wait'll Monday and tell me that," Jonah said. "You won't make any progress, you'll regress. Just like we did the other day." A disgusted breath left his lungs, sending a cloud of mist into the cold night air. "I guess I can wait a few more days for you to see that. But I won't wait forever, Silk. If I have to keep seeing you with my hands in my pockets, I'll go insane.''

''Trust me to make sure that won't happen.''

''I know it won't happen.'' All the humor left Jonah's face. ''Because I can't do it anymore, not under these conditions. I know I volunteered to do other things. But I can't keep this up. Not unless you're ready to admit the truth about us.''

''Monday, wait till—''

Jonah shook his head. ''Coward.''

The word stung like the bite of a wasp, but Carly couldn't deny it. As she gazed at him, she felt her fear growing.

She wanted to see him again, of course she did. But that's where her fear started. She couldn't let herself become dependent upon Jonah for her happiness. He was right, it was much easier to see him this way: pretending their meetings occurred nearly by chance. But if he was right about his partner, Carly wouldn't be able to pretend after next Monday.

Her shoulders slumped, remembering the determination she'd always sensed in the other woman, the possessive gleam in her tawny eyes every time she looked at Jonah or spoke of Jonah's Toys. Carly shuddered at the thought of having to tell those eyes—of having to tell herself—how she really felt about Jonah.

Carly sat on a hay bale, singing as cheerfully as she could, while trying to keep thoughts of Sylvia from dampening her joy in the season. The wind had picked up, and she longed to be indoors by a fire. Yet she hated for the evening—perhaps her last with Jonah—to end.

At last the truck turned down toward the river and stopped in front of the Moose Lodge. The little white wooden structure looked ablaze with ropes of Christmas lights along the roofline and at every window. The smell of warm sticky buns and cocoa reached them on the street, even before the front door opened.

Carly remained slumped on her hay bale while all the others left the truck. Mrs. Watson leaned heavily on Jonah as she made her way slowly up the walk. He lifted her up the stairs, but did so as unobtrusively as possible. The sight made Carly's heart swell with happiness.

A minute later he returned to the truck. "C'mon, Silk, you'll freeze to death out here."

She grinned at him. "Are you going to give me that baloney again about how you only kidnapped Mrs. Watson for singing and got her into the lodge with all her dignity intact, just as another ruse to see me?"

Jonah laughed heartily enough to warm Carly even in the bitter December wind. "No, Silk. Mrs. Watson has charms of her own. Now come have hot chocolate before your tush freezes to the hay."

Carly took his hand and climbed down. If tonight really was the last time she was ever going to see Jonah St. John, she might as well enjoy every minute of it.

Still holding her hand, Jonah escorted Carly to a chair by Mrs. Watson and went to get her cocoa. Carly looked around, relieved to see DeeDee had joined the helpers in the kitchen where she couldn't keep her eagle eye on Carly.

Mrs. Watson turned to her. "That young man gets his own way quite a bit, I'd wager," she said. "Pushes his way in, demands you do things his way. Men. They're all like that."

Carly couldn't help smiling. She could tell Mrs. Watson wasn't really angry. "I haven't known him long,

Mrs. Watson, but I'd say he usually gets what he wants one way or another.''

"You be careful, Carly," Mrs. Watson said. "He's not the sort of man to do things halfway. If you give your heart to this one, he'll demand you give it all. No holding back. And if you lose your heart to him, you'll lose the whole thing, too.''

"Lose my heart?" Carly said. "I know better than that. I keep my heart very well protected.''

Mrs. Watson regarded her over the rim of her mug. "Maybe you used to, but have you looked in a mirror recently? Seen all that glow to your complexion? Sparkle in your eyes? I can tell you right when it started, too.''

Carly was spared the problem of answering when Maizey joined them. "Well, Esther," she said. "Are you going to come back to the choir now? After tonight, everyone knows it's not your voice that keeps you at home. You sang so beautifully, I almost cried. Made us all remember how carols are supposed to sound.''

"Oh, quit the syrup, Maizey," Mrs. Watson said. "You know I can't get to church.''

Jonah returned with Carly's cocoa. Annie was with him, carrying a plate of gooey sweet rolls.

"My mom'll drive you to church, Mrs. Watson," Annie said, passing the plate to Maizey. "She won't mind.''

"And how do you think you can accomplish that, child?" Mrs. Watson said. "Did you see how Jonah got me down the steps? You can't be carrying me around like that.''

Annie looked at her feet. "I'd find a way," she mumbled.

Mrs. Watson grabbed the girl's chin and lifted her

face. "Don't mumble now, I can't hear you. Why do you care so much whether I sing?"

"I love singing, Mrs. Watson, but we can't afford lessons. I thought if we were both in the choir I could learn from you."

"Isn't there a music teacher at school?" Mrs. Watson snapped. "What's our education system coming to?"

"Oh, she's okay," said Annie. "But she's mostly into wind instruments, not voice. She said I should take lessons. And my gramma always said if I really wanted to learn to sing, I should take lessons from you."

"Your gramma?" Mrs. Watson said. "Who's your gramma?"

"Annabelle Schmidt," Annie said. "I'm named after her."

Mrs. Watson's hand began to tremble. Quickly, Carly took her mug from her before she burned herself with hot cocoa.

"Annabelle was my best friend," Mrs. Watson said.

"I know," Annie said. "Actually my whole name's Annabelle *Esther* McLaren. I'm named after you, too." She rolled her eyes. "But I never tell anyone that—it's such a *lame* name." Suddenly she realized what she'd just said to Mrs. Watson and she blushed brightly. "I'm sorry. I didn't mean—"

"Don't worry, child," Mrs. Watson said, smiling. "It is a lame name." Carly saw tears in the old woman's eyes as she gave Annie's hand a squeeze. "Annabelle's granddaughter. Last time I saw you, you were barely walking." Her lips pulled into a trembly smile. "You were a holy terror as a baby. Are you still?"

Annie blushed and looked down again. "Well, I guess...kinda."

"Good!" said Mrs. Watson.

"I could, you know, like, control it when I was singing for you. If you don't want to go to the church, I could come to your house. But—" she shot a pleading glance at Maizey and Carly "—I'm sure we could get you to the church, so everyone could hear you."

"Of course we can," Carly and Maizey said in unison.

Jonah put his hand on Mrs. Watson's shoulder. "No problem. Guaranteed."

Mrs. Watson covered her face with both hands and her shoulders shook. Jonah knelt beside her chair and spoke to her so quietly, Carly couldn't hear what he said. Mrs. Watson shook her head. He took a clean paper napkin off the table and tucked it gently between her fingers.

Mrs. Watson dabbed at her eyes, then said in a quavery voice, "I thought all my friends were dead."

"Oh, no, Esther," Maizey said. "You've got friends all over this town. Look at the friends you've got right here."

"Now don't go making me cry again, Maizey," Mrs. Watson said, with a feeble attempt at a frown.

Annie leaned over to give Mrs. Watson a kiss on her wrinkled cheek, and Carly wanted to add assurances of her own. But she couldn't say a word over the big lump of tears blocking her throat.

Jonah noticed. Grabbing another napkin with one hand and Carly's elbow with the other, he led her to the back hall. In relative privacy, he tucked her against his chest and stroked her hair.

"You are *such* a soft heart," he said.

"I'm not usually so weepy," Carly defended herself as she sniffed back tears. "I don't know what's the matter with me. It must be the season."

Jonah chuckled. "I think it was just a ploy to get me off in a private corner so you could sneak another kiss from me."

"Oh, you conceited ape," she said, her desire to cry disappearing with her smile. "Please don't do that to me again. I don't think I could...uh, stop."

"Neither could I," Jonah agreed. Smile lines around his dark eyes crinkled deeply. "Not that I think that's a reason to skip it."

"In the Moose Lodge?" Carly exclaimed. She changed the subject. "Jonah, you're liking all this Christmas stuff, aren't you? You're not really doing all this just for me."

"Oh, sure," he said. "I love going around in a half-aroused constantly frustrated state."

"But you—"

"No buts, Carly. And don't try those tears again. Mrs. Watson's great, so are your other friends. But I'm done playing Santa till you have the guts to admit your feelings to me...and to Sylvia."

"Next Monday," she said firmly. "Count on it."

Jonah's eyes roamed over her face. "I think I lied," he said.

"Lied?"

"I can stop," he said. "What do you think I am, an animal? And I don't want you in that meeting without a powerful motive to keep your word to me." His lips came closer to hers. "Besides, you know you want it."

"Of course I want you," Carly breathed, her mind spinning. "But we—"

With a confident male chuckle Jonah let his mouth and hands win the argument.

CHAPTER SEVEN

THE following weekend dragged like a dentist appointment. Gathering Christmas trees without Jonah just didn't bring the season alive for Carly.

She went with a woman who worked part-time at the gift shop and her husband. He refused to use a handsaw, declaring it a waste of time and energy. But Carly's despondency came from more than the noise of the chain saw and the businesslike way this man selected Christmas trees. The wind seemed to blow harder, the temperature never got above five, and the trees they chose all felt like they weighed tons.

As Carly dragged a particularly fat one back to the truck, she got such a stitch in her side, she had to lie down on the snow to relieve it. Gazing up at the weak winter sun and threatening clouds, she remembered how beautiful the snowstorm had looked to her last week. These clouds simply looked menacing and dark. Last week when she'd lain in the snow, a large handsome man had offered to join her there. This week…

Carly sat up and rubbed her lower back. Did she really mean to attribute all her enjoyment of the season to Jonah? *What nonsense!* She didn't need him to make the day complete. She didn't *need* him for anything.

She was just tired. It was surely the size of the trees that made her so exhausted. She grabbed the trunk again, thinking of the hot bath she'd take if she ever got out of the woods.

Sunday, Carly's normal Christmas mood reasserted itself. Of course, she didn't expect she'd have quite as much fun without Jonah. But she wasn't going to let herself get all mopey over his absence.

Actually being around him had become more difficult than pleasurable. She wouldn't describe herself—as Jonah had—as "painfully frustrated." But she spent a good part of the time she was with him admiring his strong legs and masculine buttocks, the way he used his dexterous long-fingered hands, his handsome square-jawed face with those luscious lips, set off by thick brown hair and...

Carly shook her head, wishing to rid it of such thoughts. Honestly, she remonstrated herself, she liked more about Jonah than his body. She loved his often sardonic and sometimes silly sense of humor; she loved his soft heart with little children, his unfailing instincts with women—young and old; she loved the tenderness he always showed her, even when he was hopping mad.

Stop it, Carly! she shouted silently, realizing too late where her thoughts were taking her. Did she really mean that she *loved* these things, loved *any* things, about Jonah?

Fear tensed the muscles down her spine. *Love?* Love meant trust—or it ought to. And trust was something Carly had learned not to give.

"Maizey!" Carly cried as the older woman turned into the parking lot in her ancient green pickup. "Can I ride with you?"

Maizey parked and rolled down her window. "Aren't you riding with that nice Jonah again today?"

"I don't think he's coming." Carly grabbed a tree and threw it into the back of Maizey's truck.

Maizey climbed out and looked through the trees till she found one small enough to lift herself. "Don't we usually get a man to ride with the women? Especially us *old* women?''

Carly laughed. ''Oh, we can manage, Maizey. We'll just take all these smaller trees before anyone else shows up.''

''Kids like big trees,'' Maizey grumbled.

''We'll take the biggest ones we can lift then!'' Carly snapped. Instantly she regretted her tone. ''I'm sorry, Maizey. I don't know what's the matter with me.''

''Maybe you're coming down with something,'' Maizey said. ''You look awful pale.''

''Maybe,'' Carly agreed, glad to attribute her rude behavior to the flu. ''Yesterday I got so tired I could barely drag the last tree to the truck.''

''Why don't you skip today?'' Maizey asked, resting a hand on the hood of her truck as she regarded Carly closely. ''I'm sure enough people will show up to manage. You do plenty, Carly. No one will mind if you take a day off.''

''I'll be fine.'' Carly grabbed another tree.

A car, with what looked like a dozen small children, stopped to let the driver out.

He held the door open long enough for the smell of the kids' lunch to waft out: greasy hamburgers with grilled onions. The odor must have hit Carly in the nose but it felt like a fist to her churning stomach.

She grabbed the side of Maizey's pickup and clamped her jaw shut as tight as she could, praying that she wasn't going to be sick right here. As she drew in big breaths of fresh air, another car turned in, bringing more volunteers...and more exhaust fumes.

Carly covered her mouth and nose with her mittens.

''That's it, dearie,'' said Maizey. ''You've got the bug. Now give me the lists and go on home. You don't want to make any of these people sick, do you? That'd be a fine Christmas gift.''

"Maybe you're right.''

Carly really didn't feel well enough today to deliver trees, and it didn't—she was relieved to note—have anything to do with Jonah St. John. As she dug her papers out of the file in her car, she remembered just how many kids she'd put on her list today. But it didn't matter. Maizey would never figure out that Carly had hoped— even against her better judgment—to spend another day watching Jonah bring Christmas joy to a bunch of little children.

At home, Carly built up the fire that had dwindled when DeeDee left for her day of Christmas shopping with Tommy. Neither tea nor coffee sounded good to her stomach, so she made herself a cup of cocoa. She felt so much better after that, that she made a batch of pancakes, downing several with syrup but no butter.

She took the Sunday paper and another cup of cocoa to the living room and stretched out in the old recliner in front of the woodstove. But her contentment lasted only a few minutes.

She felt a hundred times better than she had an hour ago. But in all her life she couldn't remember ever treating stomach flu by eating heartily. The only kind of nausea she ever remembered hearing about that could be cured with food was...morning sickness.

Carly leaped out of the recliner and began pacing around the room. She had obviously built up the fire far too much, for now sweat beaded on her brow. A mental camera flashed still pictures of the past month through her frantic mind.

Pictures of Carly crying over nothing, of her snapping at Jonah with barely any provocation, of her getting queasy—usually in the morning—over aromas she used to love and situations that never used to bother her. The backdrop for all the pictures was Carly's memory of the night she and Jonah met.

Running to the kitchen, she grabbed the calendar off the wall and flipped back to November to see how many days had passed since that crucial night. Nearly a month. And her last period had occurred six weeks ago.

Six weeks!

Carly knew she couldn't wait until tomorrow to get this question answered. In the morning—her heart stuttered at the thought—she had to meet with Sylvia. She had to find out before that.

Her head twirling, Carly plopped down on the kitchen stepladder. Meet with Sylvia? She pressed her hands to her temples. Tomorrow morning, she had planned to be resolute with Sylvia, to explain firmly just what her feelings were for Jonah—as if she knew!—and to refuse absolutely to go on with the mediation.

Well, the refusal part didn't sound so hard. She certainly couldn't continue *now*. But Carly couldn't quite come up with the perfect phraseology to explain why.

No, Sylvia, I'm not quite sure how I feel about Jonah. After all, we haven't known each other very long. But I am having his baby.

No, Sylvia, I can't exactly describe my relationship with Jonah, but it's a lot clearer to me now than it was the night I got pregnant by him.

Carly bit her lip, fighting tears. She knew where all this weeping came from now, but she still didn't want to give in to it. She so clearly remembered Jonah using a condom, every time. But nothing was a hundred percent successful.

Carly stared at the empty plate on the counter and

realized she'd been nibbling away at the leftover pan-cakes that she'd planned to heat in the microwave for breakfast tomorrow. After a moment's consideration, she rejected the idea of checking her weight on the bathroom scale. Enough frightening and depressing facts had hit her today, she didn't need to see another.

Grabbing her coat, Carly decided she would have to drive all the way to Bozeman to get a home pregnancy test. If she went to the local pharmacy, everyone in Wide Spot would hear about it by evening.

Besides, the drive would soothe her. A hundred and fifty miles through a beautiful canyon next to a partially frozen, rapidly rushing river was just what she needed to let her mind rest and figure out what she was going to do about this problem.

Before she'd driven fifteen minutes, Carly found she had quit thinking of her possible pregnancy as a "prob-lem." Hadn't she just this morning admitted to herself that she loved Jonah? Well, almost. When she'd gotten close to the thought, she'd run from it in fear.

It still scared her. Scared her silly. Because she knew when she admitted to loving Jonah, she would also have to recognize that she needed him. Her defenses would be breached.

Who are you kidding, Carly? her mind laughed. Her defenses had tumbled weeks ago. If she didn't love Jonah, why wasn't she praying desperately for this preg-nancy test to turn out negative? When in fact, she had to fight an urge to hope for just the opposite.

But her fear of needing another person that had seemed so enormous this morning had multiplied a hun-dredfold now. If she needed Jonah for herself, how much more did she need him with his baby inside her? And how much did that baby need him?

Carly felt a wide smile relax her face. That part didn't scare her a bit—how Jonah would feel about his baby. She'd seen him with children. He might be cynical and wisecracking with adults, but with children his heart turned to marshmallow. She began chewing her lip again and forced her thoughts back to the practical.

One thing was so clear in her mind that it never even rose as a question. Carly would keep this baby. She would raise it, hopefully with Jonah, but if not, by herself. The child had done nothing wrong, and Carly loved it already. No one would ever love it as much as she. She felt her heart swelling as she thought of cuddling it to her breast.

The baby had been conceived in love. She realized that now. The feelings of the little creature's parents since that moment weren't as clear. What would happen to them over the long term remained unanswered. But the creation of the child inside her had come from love. Carly could not, would not, let her baby down.

When she parked the car by the discount store, fear still reigned uppermost in her mind. But the decisions she had come to about her situation, and about her love for Jonah, let her enter the store with outward calm.

"Let me, Silk," Jonah said, holding the inner door open for her. "Decided to do a little Christmas shopping after all?"

Carly stared, jaw hanging. Of all people to run into now! When she'd driven seventy-five miles to avoid seeing anyone she knew.

"Silk?" Jonah waved a hand back and forth in front of her face. "Remember me? Jonah St. John?" He put out his hand to shake. "We met a few weeks ago at a Christmas party? Remember?"

"Hi, Jonah," Carly said, recovering her voice. "I was...just surprised to see you in Bozeman."

"Really?" He stepped out of the way of the other people entering the store. "I live here, people see me in Bozeman every day. It's you who's out of town."

"Right, of course. I know that." Carly gave him a weak grin. To cover her confusion, she absently pulled a shopping cart out of the stack. "I just came over..." Her words drifted to a halt.

Jonah covered her fingers on the handle of the shopping cart. "Carly, are you all right? You're acting weird."

"I'm fine, I just got a little confused because I hadn't expected to see you. You know, since you decided not to come to the Christmas tree cutting and—"

"That's right," Jonah said. "Why aren't you delivering trees with some safe, boring, married man?"

"I, uh..." Every question he asked, no matter how simple, seemed filled with hazards. What did she say now? Something about morning sickness?

"You couldn't stand it without me, could you?" He leaned toward her to whisper his words. Not close enough for intimacy. Even to tease, Jonah wouldn't embarrass her that way in the lobby of a store. Just close enough so the warmth of his breath swirled against the column of her neck as he spoke. "That's the only reason you ever did any of it this year, isn't it? To spend time with me. Admit it, Silk."

A trembly melting sensation swept through her with such ferocity, she was glad she was hanging on to the cart. "Jonah, don't do that here!" she whispered.

"Don't do what, Silk?" He gave her that ingenuous grin she didn't believe at all. "Tell you I missed you this weekend and hope you missed me?'' He put his hand over hers on the shopping cart.

"Jonah, stop it,'' Carly said. "Please. Let me think.''

Jonah straightened. "You have to think to decide if you missed me?'' he asked. "Didn't DeeDee ever tell you about the fragile male ego?''

Carly closed her eyes, grateful they had run into each other in such a public place. Her resistance to Jonah if they were in private wouldn't last a minute. Now that she thought she was carrying his child, that tomorrow at the latest she would tell him, that they might even consider getting married... She would have a very hard time even dreaming up a reason not to fall in his arms and tell him everything. Even—perhaps—that she loved him.

But here she could keep her thoughts on track. She couldn't tell Jonah now. Not a man who had wanted a child for years. She had to be sure before she even hinted he might be about to get his wish.

Besides, she didn't want to tell him until after her meeting with Sylvia. She wanted to present him with that problem cleared up before she dropped this new bombshell in his lap.

She opened her eyes. "Jonah, you always make me think such naughty thoughts, I have a hard time making sense. So please, let me get my errands done. I'm sure I'll forget something important if you're traipsing after me.''

"Traipsing, Silk?'' Jonah said, his voice sharp with annoyance. "Don't worry, I don't traipse. Not my style at all.'' He stood aside to let her walk past him with the shopping cart. As she passed, he gave her fanny a pat. "I'll just leave you to your naughty thoughts.''

She whirled on him, but he was already walking out the door. His brisk stride and stiff shoulders left her no doubt that he was angry. She didn't blame him. She hadn't handled this meeting well at all. But of course he had no idea the turmoil tangling up her thoughts. Tomorrow when she explained it all to him, he'd understand.

Two hours later, Carly examined the second spot turning pink. She had bought two tests, knowing she wouldn't be satisfied seeing the results only once. Twice was far more persuasive.

She wished now she'd told Jonah in the store. She imagined buying the tests together, waiting for the results together, being joyful together. For Carly *was* joyful, more than she would ever have dreamed. She wanted so much to know that Jonah was joyful, too. She had to tell him.

She telephoned him, hoping she could get him to drive over tonight to Wide Spot. She didn't want to tell him over the phone. But after her blundering at the store, he might still be angry enough that he wouldn't want to make the long drive unless she gave him a good reason. In the end, she didn't have to decide how much to give away on the phone, because his answering machine picked up the phone.

Disconsolately, Carly sat at the kitchen table while night fell, getting up only to fetch snacks. When she heard Tommy's pickup turn into the gift shop parking lot below, she leaped up. She couldn't face DeeDee now. Grabbing the paraphernalia from the tests, she stuffed it all at the bottom of the wastebasket, and ran to her bedroom.

If Carly had been nervous about her meeting with Sylvia last week, this morning she was petrified. Sylvia was so…demanding. When she asked questions, Carly felt like a hostile witness under cross-examination by a killer lawyer.

Could she possibly keep her pregnancy secret from Sylvia? Especially when Carly was determined to tell the woman everything else, if necessary, to convince her that she was withdrawing as mediator.

She had no doubt that if Sylvia found out about the baby, *she*, not Carly, would be the one who got to tell Jonah. And all Carly's expected joy in that moment would be stolen.

Not surprisingly, Sylvia tried to take control the moment she arrived. "I think this will work much better," she said, hanging up her coat. "Just the two of us. No structure."

Carly started to offer coffee, but Sylvia shook her head.

"I'm trying to cut down on caffeine." She sat in the chair she always took. "Let me explain why I wanted this meeting. You see, something's happened that changes…well, *everything*."

"Sylvia, I'm not sure I should hear this," Carly said. "If I'm withdrawing, wouldn't you rather explain this to your new mediator?"

"No," Sylvia said. "This is about you. You see, after Jonah and I saw you the first time, things began to get better between us."

"I thought you said you'd made no progress."

"In the business dispute, we didn't," Sylvia said. She twisted her gold bracelet around her wrist. "But all the talking helped us personally. That's why I was so angry the other day."

Carly frowned, confused. "Do you think you can't

make progress with another mediator?'' she asked. ''That's not—''

''No.'' Sylvia cut her off. ''I was concerned about the personal relationship *you* want to develop with Jonah.''

Carly drew in a breath. She had to explain now; she couldn't let Sylvia go on without knowing how Carly felt.

Sylvia must have read her mind; she made a slashing gesture with her palm. ''Please, let me finish.'' She drew circles with her red lacquered nail on the arm of her chair. ''You see, I'm going to have Jonah's baby.''

Carly's heart quit beating. She knew it did because she couldn't breathe. Her head spun dizzily. A sharp pain began in the center of her chest and spread until it seemed to engulf all of her.

''Have...uh...'' Carly sucked in air. ''Do you mean you're...pregnant?''

''No,'' Sylvia said. ''I don't think so. Not yet.'' She lowered her gaze to her manicured hands. ''Well... we haven't used...protection this month. I'm sure it will happen any day.'' She turned her tawny eyes back on Carly. ''And I can hardly wait to see Jonah's face when I tell him that now I want a baby as much as he does.''

Carly opened her mouth, but the ache in her throat kept her from speaking. *Sylvia* wanted to watch Jonah's face light up with joy? Carly had spent the night dreaming of just that moment. Jonah said he'd wanted a baby for years. He must have wanted it more than Carly had guessed, since he seemed to be...distributing his seed generously. He'd gotten one woman pregnant and one planning to be at any minute.

Which must also mean...it *had* to mean...he had taken two women to his bed.

A wave of nausea wrenched Carly's stomach. She

longed for solitude to make sense of her feelings. At the moment, the universe felt upside down.

"Are you sure..." she finally managed, then stopped herself.

She couldn't ask Sylvia if she was sure of Jonah's feelings. That would sound so...desperate. If he didn't love Sylvia, what was he doing in her bed? With more strength than she thought she had, Carly forced hurt and anger from her mind.

"Are you sure this is right for you, Sylvia?" she asked. "You always said you didn't want children."

"I know I did." Sylvia's smile lit her face in a way Carly would never have believed possible. "I had no idea I would react this way when I finally made up my mind. I've never been so happy. I'm just filled with joy over it, I wish I had done it years ago." She wiped at her cheek as if dashing away a tear. "I want to tell him Christmas morning, to make it the most special Christmas we've had in years. Maybe ever. I just know how happy it will make him."

Carly's jaw ached from clamping so tightly. "Yes, it certainly will." Her voice sounded hollow to her ears, but Sylvia didn't seem to notice. Or maybe she just didn't care. "Happy, yes...just what he's always wanted."

Yesterday, *she* had thought *her* news would make Jonah wildly happy. She had even wondered if he would want to marry her for their baby's sake. *Marriage!* What a joke that would seem to a man with two lovers.

Thank God she hadn't had a chance to tell Jonah and make a total fool of herself. Heat throbbed in her cheeks at the thought of the telephone conversation they would have had last night if she'd gotten through to him.

Sylvia looked down at her hands in her lap. "I'm sure

you can see now, Carly, why I wanted to meet with you this morning.'' She looked up, her expression devoid of anything but sweet joy. "I just want a chance to tell him my own way."

"Of *course* I won't tell him anything," Carly exclaimed. "I won't ever reveal anything we say here to each other. It's all confidential unless you talk about it. Saying anything would violate everything that's important about mediation."

Sylvia looked satisfied that Carly was speaking the truth. "I don't mean just that," she said. "I want, need, a few more weeks to put my relationship with Jonah back together. To get a chance to tell him about…our having a baby together without…outside pressures undermining my chances."

"Outside pressures?" Carly asked icily. "You mean me?"

"Yes," Sylvia said. "If you're honest, you'll admit that's what you are. I don't want to tell Jonah about my change of heart when he's feeling ambivalent. I don't want him to marry me just to have a baby. I want him to come to me freely, then tell him about wanting to get pregnant. That's the other reason I want to wait till Christmas morning."

"I… Christmas…"

"That's not very long, Carly," Sylvia said. "A couple of weeks. I don't think that's much to ask. Really, you know, you should never have taken on this mediation. You were conflicted right from the beginning, and you certainly weren't honest about that. Not with me."

"I never meant to be dishonest, Sylvia," Carly said. "I had no relationship with Jonah at the time, we had only met once. I simply…" She stopped talking, realizing she had no desire to explain anything to Sylvia.

And no need to. She could easily promise Sylvia the few weeks of silence she asked for. In fact, she would give her a lifetime. For after what she had just learned, Carly had no intention of ever seeing Jonah St. John again as long as she lived.

She had spent the past six weeks falling in love with him. He had obviously spent the time satisfying his desires with another woman, while teasing Carly's emotions into full blown love. A love that must mean nothing to him. And for all she knew, what he felt for Sylvia went far beyond lust. Maybe the kind of love she felt for Jonah was exactly what he felt for Sylvia.

After all, he hadn't used protection with *Sylvia*, and he'd never failed to do so with Carly. Just because nature had gotten things backward didn't mean Jonah hadn't made it perfectly clear which woman he *wanted* to bear his children.

Well, it didn't matter. Carly would never find out anything more ever about Jonah's emotions. She would never have another conversation with him about anything personal. She'd survived betrayal before, she could do so again. No matter that she had let her heart be slashed to ribbons, at least she still had her dignity.

Praying for self-control, Carly pulled her mediator's cloak over her. "Sylvia," Carly said. "My understanding is that you're asking me not to pursue a relationship with Jonah, at least until after Christmas when you get a chance to tell him about your wish to have his child."

"Yes," Sylvia said. "Give me a chance to—"

"Fine," Carly interrupted, ignoring the cardinal rule of mediation. "I have no intention of doing any such thing. Believe me, I would never try to come between a man and his child. It would violate more than my mediator's code of ethics. I...wouldn't be able to live with myself.''

A broad smile slowly spread across Sylvia's attractive face, softening even the assessing look in her catlike eyes. ''Thank you, Carly,'' she said tearily. ''You've made me so happy. In fact, when he hears about it, I'm sure Jonah will think the same thing. We owe our happiness together to you.''

CHAPTER EIGHT

CARLY sat in her mediation office for over an hour after Sylvia left, struggling not to cry, not to get sick, most of all, not to drive to Bozeman and confront Jonah with his duplicity.

But she couldn't do that. As she had told Sylvia, revealing anything she learned in a mediation session would violate everything she believed in. She simply couldn't. Nor could she tell Jonah about the baby *she* was carrying.

Sylvia was right. Carly shouldn't have taken this mediation. When she did, she committed herself to certain things. She hadn't actually violated any of her personal rules or ethics. After all, she hadn't gotten pregnant while she was mediating this dispute.

But she had led Sylvia into a dreadful position. Sylvia had risked pregnancy trying to restore her relationship with Jonah, something she wouldn't even have attempted if it hadn't been the things Carly had brought out during mediation. She had done so with the absolute confidence—a confidence she was entitled to have—that no matter how many other women she might be competing with for Jonah's love, Carly wasn't one of them.

Carly couldn't now go to Jonah and…what was the term? Alienate his affection. If Sylvia was right that she had a chance to put her relationship with Jonah back together, Carly had to give her the space to do so. As she had said, she wouldn't come between them.

Carly was used to taking care of herself. She would

take care of her baby herself, also. She prayed it was a girl, so she could start teaching her right away about the unfaithfulness of males. Carly had learned a lot from her father growing up. Too bad she had let herself forget his most important lesson—even for one night.

That wouldn't happen to *her* child. *Her* child would grow up independent and strong and…Carly's chin quivered…lonely.

Leaning her head on her arms, she allowed herself to sob. She had earned these tears. Tomorrow she would be strong.

She'd have to be.

Even if she *could* tell Jonah now, she wouldn't. What rational independent woman would want a man who would bed two women?

Carly continued crying, avoiding an answer to that question. Because she knew she did. She had never wanted anything as much as she wanted Jonah St. John. Because—she might as well admit the rest of it—she had never loved anyone the way she loved Jonah St. John.

Carly stood and retrieved the box of tissues from the shelf in the corner. Wiping her eyes and blowing her nose, she commanded herself to get a grip. If Jonah loved her, he would come back to her even after Sylvia's announcement.

Love, Carly? her mind mocked. If Jonah loved her, would he have been sleeping with another woman?

Drawing in a long, shuddery breath, Carly tried to fill herself with the kind of resolve she used to feel—*before* she'd met Jonah St. John. She had been alone for years: by choice.

So she had made a mistake with Jonah, let her heart's defenses down for the first time in years. That should simply add to her store of knowledge about men and duplicity. She would arm herself with that knowledge and never get into this situation again.

Situation. Now there was a word. Most people, listening to Carly's tale of woe, would assume she meant her pregnancy. But Carly knew better. The situation she had every intention of avoiding the rest of her life was this terrible, needful, all-consuming love.

In fact, it was that very love that made her most sure she wouldn't do or say a thing to intrude between Jonah and Sylvia. They had a relationship of many years standing. He had obviously loved her enough to ask her to marry him. He had wanted to spend the rest of his life with her, wanted her to be the mother of his children.

He had never said any of those things to Carly. If he could find happiness with Sylvia again, with the family they would have together, Carly wouldn't even want to interfere. Much as she wished he returned *her* love, if Jonah decided his happiness lay elsewhere, she would let him go without a word. She loved him too much to do anything else.

Carly sighed and began straightening the office, glad of the strength and independence she had gained since her father's death. If Tommy ever convinced DeeDee to marry him, Carly and the baby could live in the apartment upstairs. Years from now, when Carly finally finished paying off her father's debts, maybe she could afford a little house for her and her child.

She would be fine. Her baby would be fine. Splashing water in her face to remove all trace of tears, Carly went to work her shift at the gift shop.

Tuesday night with a heavy heart, Carly dug out her list of which trees still needed decorating. There were only nine left, which was lucky, since she wasn't sure how many people would actually show up tonight. The closer the day got to Christmas, the harder it was to get people to take time from their own families.

And tree decorating couldn't be done as quickly as many of the other chores. Usually each volunteer did only one a night.

When she heard people begin to arrive in the parking lot, Carly went downstairs, relieved to see so many. She was counting heads when Jonah's bright red pickup turned into the lot. Even in the dark, Carly recognized it.

She stared, then realized she had lost count of who went to which tree. "Where were we?" she said to Maizey.

"You just told me Andersen's tree," Maizey said. "But you hadn't picked anyone to go with me."

Carly's eyes remained on Jonah as he walked toward the group huddled by the back door out of the wind. "Well, why don't you go with Maizey, Jonah?" she said brightly. "Mrs. Andersen got a huge tree, her grandchildren like a big one, and we need someone tall to reach the top branches."

During this too cheerful speech, Jonah's eyes narrowed and his shoulders grew stiff. "Andersen's tree?" he said, his voice tight.

Carly finished assigning the volunteers, shivering under Jonah's angry gaze. With her teeth chattering, she stumbled several times over names and addresses. But she was sure everyone else attributed her stuttering to the cold.

As the others began to disperse, Jonah said, "Better get in the car out of the cold, Maizey. I'll join you in a minute. I need to talk to Carly."

Carly stood in silence watching Maizey walk to her car, then spoke quickly before Jonah could begin. "We don't need to talk right now, do we, Jonah?" she said, her lips growing stiff from the cold. "Maizey needs to get home and—"

"What I want to talk about," Jonah interrupted, "is what *we* need. Why the hell didn't you call me yesterday after your meeting with Sylvia? And what is this crap about decorating trees with Maizey? You know damn well why I come over here, and it's not to decorate Christmas trees."

"Call you after my meeting?" Carly pulled her jacket tighter. "Jonah, everything said in that meeting was confidential. I can't tell you anything we said."

"I don't care what you *said*," Jonah muttered. "I care about the outcome." He turned up gloved palms. "Which was?"

"If you mean, am I still your mediator, I'm not."

"Good." Jonah took her arm. "Then you can come with Maizey and me tonight."

"I'm going to a different house tonight," Carly said, pulling her arm free. "There was one house left and... Well, Maizey doesn't like to go alone and.... And I...couldn't go with you anyway. I agreed with Sylvia that I wouldn't have any more...contact with you until the two of you solve your problems."

"Solve?" His eyes narrowed. "And who gets to define that?"

"You two get to define it," Carly said. "Together."

"What the hell's going on, Carly?" Jonah sounded hurt, angry hurt. And confused. "What happened to you? Where's the woman who kissed me on the caroling truck last week? The woman who swore she'd get free of this mediation so she could see me?"

"Jonah, there are people waiting for us," Carly said. "We can't talk about this now."

"Quit hiding behind that stuff, Carly," Jonah snapped. "You've spent too many years being bitter over your father's death, being noble." He kicked a lump of frozen gravel and ice. "Paying his debts when you don't have to, blaming every man you meet for his betrayal. Stop it. Stop it right now tonight." He pulled her to him. "You need this, too."

With wrenching self-denial, Carly turned her face away from Jonah's seeking lips, wondering when he last tried to kiss Sylvia this way. "What I need is to fulfill my obligations."

Jonah released her, shaking his head. "When you were alone, Silk, all this charity may have been all right. It was probably a nice distraction for you to hide behind."

Carly felt as if he'd slapped her. "Distraction? Is that all you think this is? These people need help, and there's nothing wrong with that."

"Not a thing," Jonah agreed. "No one suggested there was. But what about me? Do I have to get on one of your lists to see you? Giving all this time to everyone else now…it's selfish. Self-centered. Glorifying yourself at my expense. *Our* expense." He jabbed his finger toward her. "What about *your* needs, Silk?"

"My needs are met just fine."

"Ri-ight," Jonah said sardonically. "That why you seduced me the night we met?"

"Seduced *you*?" Carly exclaimed.

"Damn right," Jonah said. "You were so needy and wanting, it radiated off you."

Carly's bottom lip trembled violently as she fought back tears. That night was what Jonah remembered about her. That night was what he wanted to repeat. But when Carly tried to remember it now, the woman her mind showed her in Jonah's loving arms was Sylvia.

"That was a moment of weakness, Mr. St. John, one that won't be repeated." She tried to turn away.

"Think about *my* needs then, damn it." Jonah grabbed her arm and pulled her to face him.

Carly lifted her chin. "We both *need* to decorate trees for the people who are waiting for us."

Jonah's hand tightened slowly on her arm. Then he released her with a disgusted oath. "Too bad your father *isn't* still around, Silk. He could warm your selfish little backside."

With that, he spun on his heel and strode to his truck. Jerking open the door, he stood a moment with his foot on the floorboard. Carly held her breath. Did Jonah really mean to just drive off, leaving Maizey and Carly to decorate two trees themselves?

Not that she would blame him. He'd come a long way over icy roads tonight with something else entirely in mind than spending the evening with Maizey VanDorn. So why would it surprise her for Jonah to go back on his word? He'd certainly done exactly that making love to Sylvia while pretending to be interested in Carly.

And yet it *would* surprise her. She felt very strongly that Jonah wouldn't drive off in a huff, not after promising to help.

Jonah cursed, slammed his truck door and strode over to Maizey's car. Carly's muscles relaxed with such suddenness, she almost sat down on the porch step. But she forced herself to walk to her car. She had a tree to decorate, as well—thank God.

Perhaps if she concentrated very hard on where to put

each Christmas ball, she could forget her confusing ambivalent thoughts about Jonah St. John for a few hours.

That Friday evening, Carly and DeeDee arrived first at the high school lunchroom to help prepare gallons of turkey stuffing and peel hundreds of potatoes. In prior years, Carly had enjoyed this night of getting ready for the Community Christmas Dinner as much as the dinner itself. She was determined to do so tonight, as well.

As long as she didn't have to chop the onions for the stuffing, nor sauté them in butter. In fact, she hoped to get far enough away from the stove that she couldn't smell the onions cooking, though in a crowded kitchen that was a slim hope.

Her stomach lurched thinking about it.

DeeDee gave her an odd look. "Are you all right, Carly? You've been acting funny all week." She put a hand to her daughter's forehead. "If you're sick, you shouldn't cook food the rest of the town's going to eat."

"I'm fine, Mom," Carly assured her. "It's just that time of the month." She opened one of the cupboards and began pulling out big aluminum tubs to mix the stuffing in.

DeeDee continued to regard her closely. "Is Jonah coming tonight?"

"I have no idea," Carly said. "He doesn't tell me his plans, you know. But my guess would be no. What men ever come to help us cook?"

"Tommy's coming," DeeDee said. She smiled as she laid out vegetable parers and mixing spoons. "He's our best potato peeler."

"One in a million," Carly said, glad to change the subject to her mother's love life. "Why don't you marry him?"

DeeDee laughed. "Maybe I will." Her smile didn't fade but her voice turned serious. "How does New Year's day sound to you?"

"Really, Mom?" Carly squealed, hugging her mother fiercely, crushing a spoon between them in her glee. "New Year's. I'm so happy for you."

DeeDee looked relieved. "Are you really, dear? Tommy and I talked about it a lot, you know. I haven't wanted to leave you alone. But we think you'll be all right now. You know, with Jonah and—"

"Jonah?" Carly asked. "What does he have to do with you getting married?"

"I was too worried about you before," DeeDee said. "I was afraid you'd spend the rest of your life alone, inside that little walled fortress you built around your emotions. But now that Jonah—"

"Mom," Carly interrupted again. "Jonah and I are not...well, we're not like you and Tommy or anything. You're reading too much into things."

DeeDee shook her head. "Even if you don't end up with Jonah, I think you'll be all right now. Even if you never see him again, at least he broke through...into your heart. You'll start to feel again now. It would be too painful to stop once you've started again. You've been so happy the last month."

"Really?" Carly said, her voice cracking. The anguish of the past days seemed so much more immediate to her.

"Did you think you could hide it from me?" DeeDee said. "I'm your mother!"

"I guess not," Carly said, forcing a smile. "Just don't start counting on a double wedding in January."

"I'm not that pushy," DeeDee said. She pretended to

consider it. "Though maybe if I spoke to Jonah..." She let her words trail off.

"Mom, you wouldn't!"

"Of course I wouldn't." DeeDee laughed. She dumped two sacks of potatoes into one of the deep sinks. "When did I ever embarrass you with one of your boyfriends?"

Carly shook her head, laughing, too. "I can't count that high," she said.

Her happiness for her mother, though it didn't quite calm Carly's stomach, took her mind off her own problems. It also helped that she and Tommy ended up peeling potatoes together.

They joked and laughed and felt closer than they had before. The realization that this kind, loving man would be her child's grandfather filled Carly with comfortable joy. She was unreservedly happy for her mother.

And though DeeDee was wrong in thinking that Carly and Jonah were a couple, she was certainly right that Carly wouldn't be alone anymore. Not for the next twenty years or so till her baby was raised.

"Maizey, answer the phone, will you?" Carly heard someone say. "Your hands are clean."

Maizey grabbed the phone. "Yes, yes, we are... Oh, about the same as last year, I'd guess... Good heavens, no! Why we won't have enough... Oh, well that's good... And merry Christmas to you, too."

Maizey hung up the phone. "We're going to have a lot more people this year," she said. "That was the minister from the Presbyterian church. He said the whole choir and the ladies' auxiliary are coming tomorrow—and bringing all their families."

"Why, that'll be more than a hundred extra people!" DeeDee exclaimed.

"I know," Maizey said. "But he said someone has donated a dozen fresh turkeys, with all the trimmings, and they're bringing them over right now." She fluttered her hands through the air. "I'll go let them in."

"Who donated all that food?" Carly asked. "And why didn't they let us know earlier? We'll be here all night!"

"He didn't say who donated it," Maizey said, taking the keys off the hook above the phone. "But isn't this what you've always wanted for this dinner, Carly? To have everyone in town come."

"Oh, yes," Carly said, wishing she could explain that it was just the onions that worried her. "I think it's wonderful. I wish all the churches were doing the same thing."

And she did, she told herself at 2:00 a.m., when she finally left the school kitchen to go home. Though her back ached unmercifully, she wished even more people would come tomorrow. Especially one more person whom she didn't expect to see at all.

She wondered if he'd have peeled potatoes as efficiently as Tommy. Probably not, since Jonah hadn't been in the army. At least, she didn't think he had. He'd never mentioned it. She really knew so little about him. What would she tell his child about him when she— Carly had firmly decided now that the baby would be a girl—asked about her father?

Refusing a ride from Maizey, Carly walked the few blocks to her apartment in the beautiful cold night, looking at the thick wash of stars overhead. Growing up in a city, she'd rarely seen stars. What a gift to give her child, this nightly view of the heavens.

The thought of stars and heavens and Christmas and a baby growing inside her filled Carly with the peace and joy she should feel in the season…and in the coming event. She wished desperately that she could share the joy with Jonah. But whether she could or not, she would never again think of this baby as anything other than a joyful event.

Especially after her morning sickness went away.

Just before the onslaught the next afternoon, Carly began setting the lunchroom tables with donated Christmas tablecloths. The smell of roasting turkey filled the room, making her mouth water. She wondered if she'd have time for a snack before…

Giggling sounds came from the hall and she looked up to see two little girls running through the double doors with a homemade poster. They ran up to the stage at the end of the lunchroom and put the sign on an easel.

In bright Christmas colors, it read Christmas Music By The Two Esthers. Carly stared, reading it over, wondering if it really meant what she thought.

Maizey came up behind her. "Surprised?"

"Maizey," Carly said. "Does that really mean Annie and Mrs. Watson?"

"You bet it does," Maizey said. "That's why half the church is coming. Esther and Annie have been practicing with the choir. Gonna sing this week in church, too."

"But how will they get here?" Carly said. "Do I need to go pick up Mrs. Watson? How did she get to church to practice?"

Maizey gave her a huge smile. "You had your head under a rock, Carly? Town got a brand new wheelchair access van this week. It's got this electric ramp or something—haven't seen it myself—that goes over steps so they're not a problem. Gets Esther down her steps and up the ones at the church. On her own. Well, nearly.

Annie helps her quite a bit, I guess. But she does it with a walker, not a wheelchair.''

''But…but…'' Carly stared at the forks she was holding in her hand. ''Where did it come from?''

Now Maizey looked confused. ''You really don't know? Why that saint of a man, Jonah, gave it to the town. Said it had something to do with a bet with you.''

''Bet?'' Carly said weakly.

''Finish those tables,'' DeeDee called from the kitchen. ''We need to start serving.''

Carly hurried through the rest of the tables and took her place at the serving line. She longed for an hour alone to think things through, but with four hundred people for dinner, solitude was impossible.

While she chatted and served half the town, her tumbling thoughts reached only one conclusion: her picture of Jonah needed completing. Tuesday she had been as sure as she was of the sunrise that Jonah wouldn't walk off and leave Maizey after he'd promised to help. Yet moments before her conviction that he had betrayed her with Sylvia had kept her from kissing him, despite her body's longing for the contact.

She even found herself wondering if he might show up today. He *had* signed up to serve. Of course she didn't really think he would, not after Tuesday night. But she realized that some deep not clearly recognized part of her brain had decided Jonah *was* trustworthy, no matter how many women he was bedding.

No, it wasn't her brain at all. It was her heart that knew that. That was why she'd fallen in love with him. Because she trusted him.

How did that fit with his betrayal? He was skeptical, even mocking sometimes…and softhearted and loving. He—

"Carly, can I have seconds on mashed potatoes?"

No wonder she had solved nothing by the time the music began.

Mrs. Watson and Annie didn't need an introduction. The roar of hundreds of happy mealtime conversations quieted in seconds when their two voices joined to sing "Silent Night."

Carly understood then why the whole church had come to hear them. When she first saw the poster, she had expected that everyone would sing with them. But no one did. No one moved, no one whispered. No one wanted to miss a second of the beautiful music these two voices created.

Carly's chest ached, she longed so intensely for Jonah to share this moment with her. This was his gift to the town, his gift to Mrs. Watson and Annie. But Carly's bitterness last time she'd seen him had kept him away from the dinner. In doing so, she had deprived him of the joy he deserved to feel right now.

Thunderous applause filled the lunchroom. Carly knew she should start cutting pumpkin pies, but she couldn't tear her eyes from Mrs. Watson's obvious pleasure at the response of their audience. Annie whispered to her and they began another carol.

As Carly was wishing for the hundredth time that her biology had produced another hormone to remind her she was pregnant besides the one that made her cry over everything, she heard a deep voice behind her.

"Silk," Jonah whispered, "I've got someone here I'd like you to meet."

Dabbing her eyes quickly with a dish towel, Carly spun around and saw Jonah with a woman she'd have recognized anywhere. Her dark eyes sparkled like Jonah's, her thick brown hair looked even lusher than his, hanging down below her shoulders in gorgeous waves. The hand she extended to shake was slender but long-fingered and strong, just like Jonah's.

"You have to be Tory!" Carly said, sure of that though she wasn't sure of much else at the moment. What on earth was Jonah doing here? Hadn't he been furious last time he'd seen her?

"Women," Jonah said. "Do you have to do that intuition thing?"

Tory smiled at Carly. The fan lines around her eyes were more pronounced than Jonah's, no doubt from all her outdoor work in the sun. "I'm glad to meet you, Carly," she said softly.

"How did you know it was Tory?" Jonah asked.

"You're kidding, right?" Carly said, commanding herself to keep things light. "Her voice is the only thing different from you. At least as far as appearances go."

"My voice?" Tory asked.

"Mmm-hmm," Carly said. "It's so soft. Undemanding. Questioning rather than autocratic." She stopped because she and Tory were giggling.

"I forgot to tell you about her rotten sense of humor," Jonah said, with a mock frown at Carly.

"I wanted to meet you," Tory said, "to thank you."

Carly frowned. "Thank me?" she asked. "Whatever for?"

"For sending Jonah back to us," Tory said.

"Me!" Carly said. "I didn't do anything." She transferred her gaze to Jonah. "He did that on his own."

"Not according to him," Tory said.

"Jonah?" Carly said, confused. She wished they were alone, and she thanked God they were not. "What—"

"I got Tory up before dawn to get here in time," he said, glancing at the heated serving tables. "Do you think there's enough food left for her to have dinner?"

was imperceptible, at least to me. I didn't even see my-self coming to believe that. I just one day…did.'' He gave Carly a look of gratitude. ''You convinced me I was nuts.''

''I didn't say that.''

''Not in so many words,'' Jonah said. ''You just made me remember that Tory is too damn honest for her own good.'' He shrugged and leaned back in his chair. ''And watching you do all these things for your town reminded me how much I used to enjoy giving away my toys. I'd just forgotten.''

Tory smiled. ''I don't care how it happened, Carly, I'm just glad. And believe me, your timing was perfect.''

''What do you mean?'' Carly asked.

''I'm getting married this summer,'' Tory said. ''I've kind of put it off for a while.''

Jonah made a noise of disbelief. ''For five years,'' he said. ''Poor Hank, I don't know why he stuck with you.''

Tory grinned unrepentantly. ''I don't, either,'' she laughed. ''But we've waited so long, he thinks we ought to start a family right away.'' Her grin faded. ''Well, not *immediately*, but, you know, soon. I'm not easy with kids the way Jonah is. Whole idea scares me to death. But I feel a lot better about it now that good ol' Uncle Jonah's back.''

''I've seen you with kids,'' Jonah said. ''Better stick to the cows, let Hank take care of the babies.''

''Funny,'' Tory said, but she gave Jonah a look filled with love. ''Have you seen him with children?'' she asked Carly, aiming a thumb at her brother.

Carly nodded as poignant memories of Jonah deliv-ering Christmas trees to kids came rushing back to her. She wanted desperately to change the direction of this conversation before she said something too revealing about Jonah and children. But a mental picture of Jonah with a newborn baby was strangling her voice.

"I...yes," she finally managed.

"Well, you know why I feel better then," Tory said. "I mean...if you were pregnant, wouldn't you be glad to know a man like Jonah was going to be around a lot?"

Heat rushed into Carly's face, only to drain away a second later. Her mind screamed at her to answer Tory's question truthfully.

But she couldn't, because Jonah wasn't going to be around her baby—*his* baby. He was going to be too busy raising the one he would have with Sylvia. And, it sounded like, visiting his sister and her new baby.

Have a man like Jonah around a lot? Carly would be glad if Jonah would simply acknowledge her baby. But that wasn't going to happen, either.

Carly kept her hands wrapped tightly around her coffee mug so Jonah and his sister couldn't see them trembling. She had no idea how long she sat staring at Tory, not answering her question. But she had a terrible fear that if she spoke at all, she would reveal all the things she was committed not to tell.

Another round of applause sounded from the lunchroom. Then, at the urging of Annie, everyone began singing together at last.

"Oh thank heav... I mean, oh, dear," Carly said. "I've got to go cut pies."

Praying her quaking knees would support her, Carly fled.

CHAPTER NINE

CARLY "hid" at the sink, washing roasting pan after roasting pan, till the skin on her hands felt shriveled as a prune. But she wouldn't leave the sink until she knew Jonah and his sister had left the school. Conversation grew quieter around her, but Carly kept her focus on her chosen task.

"You're done, Carly," Jonah said. "Everything's clean. I'll give you a ride home."

Carly turned and saw that her plan had backfired. She and Jonah were the only two people left in the kitchen. "Where's Mom?" she asked. "And—"

"I told them all we'd finish up," Jonah said. "They went home."

"Tory?"

"I sent her to the motel," Jonah said. "She was tired from the drive."

Carly looked around the sparkling kitchen. "I guess that's it." She darted into the cloakroom. "I'll just get my coat."

Jonah followed her, took her coat from her hands and held it for her. "We're going to talk, Carly. You can't put it off forever. What's wrong with now?"

"I'm so tired from all this," Carly said. *And from growing a baby inside me.* "I didn't get much sleep last night, we didn't get done till long after midnight. I just want to go home and stretch out by a fire."

"Good idea," Jonah said. "We can talk there. C'mon, I've got my car."

"Okay," Carly said. "But we can't talk about much with Mom there."

"She won't be there," Jonah said. "She's over at Tommy's, planning their wedding I understand. She agreed with me that a talk like that would take several hours."

"You banished my mother from her own house?" Carly tried to sound annoyed.

In fact, Jonah's determination was making her more nervous than angry. He wanted an explanation she just couldn't give, not without violating a confidence and a commitment.

"Jonah, didn't you understand what I said last week?" she asked him. "I can't...see you until you and Sylvia—"

"Damn it, Silk!" Jonah said. "*You're* the one who doesn't understand. Sylvia will never agree that our problems are solved. She'll never let this end while she thinks you're a threat to her. And, trust me, that's what she's decided."

"I won't let her control my whole life, Jonah," Carly said. She stopped at the door to the hall and poked him in the chest. "Besides, Mr. St. John, *you* got us into this tangle as much as I did. Sylvia had no idea what she was getting into. Because of that we both owe her a little time to straighten out—"

"She's manipulating you," Jonah said disgustedly. "And *you're* letting her do it. She's got you acting like you're her puppet. You're obeying all her unreasonable demands, and for all I know, you're suggesting some of your own!"

"I am *not*!" Carly snapped.

How dare Jonah say Sylvia was pulling *her* strings? *He* was the one who'd made love to the woman. Every time she started to let herself feel close to Jonah again that essential fact loomed in her thoughts.

Jonah paused and seemed to swallow his annoyance. "I'm sorry, Silk. I just... Don't you even give a damn whether we see each other again?"

"Of course I care," Carly said. She didn't add, *I just wonder if you'll still care after next Friday morning*.

Jonah took her arm and started toward the doors to the parking lot. Halfway down the hall, he realized she was nearly trotting to keep up with him, and he slowed his steps. "Why do you think I came here today, Silk?"

"I've been trying to figure that out," Carly said. "Last Tuesday, you were so angry, I was sure I'd never see you again." She faced him as he held the door open for her. "I felt so bad today when Mrs. Watson and Annie started singing and you weren't there to hear that beautiful performance. You did so much to make it happen. I felt I'd kept you from hearing them."

"Don't worry, we heard most of it," Jonah said, following her outside. He didn't speak again until they were in his car with the heater going. "I didn't plan to see you again after Tuesday. I figured you had made up your mind that getting close to any man ever again was so risky, you just wouldn't do it. That trust was not a word in your vocabulary."

"I used to feel that way," Carly said. "I had good reason to." She briefly covered Jonah's hand on the gearshift. "But I don't think it's true anymore."

"I don't, either," Jonah said. "That's what confused me. Then I figured it out on the drive home to see Tory. I realized how much Sylvia had influenced me over the years. I don't think she even does it consciously. She's just...not very confident. She'll do whatever it takes to feel secure in her life. In my case, she feels most secure if she's the only person in my life I really trust.''

''Insecure,'' Carly said, shaking her head. ''That's so different from the impression she gives when you meet her.''

''I know,'' Jonah said. ''But it's her basic makeup.'' He pulled into the parking lot next to the gift shop and turned off the motor. ''C'mon, I'll build that fire for you.''

''I can manage, Jonah,'' Carly protested, though she had a feeling it was useless to say so.

The conversation had seemed quite manageable on the quick drive home. She didn't know what would happen when she and Jonah were alone in her apartment. Her promise to Sylvia nagged at her guilt feelings. And her promise to herself, not to allow herself to count on a man who loved two women at once, seemed even more at risk.

For she did trust Jonah. It made no sense, but she did. She wasn't sure exactly how it had happened. But it didn't mean that she wanted to *need* him. She had to prevent herself from falling into that trap: needing a man who would start building a family with another woman in a few days' time.

Renewing her resolve to keep herself safe, Carly let Jonah follow her upstairs. She hung her coat on a hook by the back door, giving nothing more than a resigned sigh when Jonah hung his there, too. Without another word, he built up the fire in the woodstove till its crackling heat was filling every corner of the room.

Carly watched him, wishing she could change into soft old sweats or her thick down robe. But she didn't want to take off her clothes with Jonah in the house. She decided to stay in her jeans, though they'd grown uncomfortably tight recently.

Jonah shut the door to the woodstove and stood. When he turned to gaze at her, the warmth in his dark eyes, the desire he took no trouble to hide, lit an answering flame in Carly. Her resolution slipped so abruptly she wondered if he heard the crash.

Everything in her acknowledged how glad she was to see him, how glad she was he'd come to the dinner and heard the singing. How glad she was, in fact, that she'd met him that night in Bozeman—the night that had started all his Christmas giving.

The night that had started their baby. She was glad of that, too. She only wished she could tell him so.

Jonah must have read her eyes as easily as she read his. Without a word, he took one long stride and pulled her into his arms. Crushing her to him, he sought her lips, hungrily, fiercely.

"I need you, Carly," he moaned against her mouth. "It's been too long." His hand slid down her back, cupping her buttocks, pulling her tight into the vee of his legs.

The feel of his hardening response to her made her groan; she couldn't hold it back. She arched and sighed and almost cried with her desire to take Jonah inside her, her desire to tell him about his child in her womb. Opening her mouth, she received his tongue and offered hers.

Desire swept through her, from her aching center to every welcoming part of her body. It swiftly encompassed her mind and heart. The intimate sensations she craved entwined indelibly with her emotions. She would never feel these physical things with another man, for no other man would ever capture her heart.

If only she could believe Jonah shared these special touches with no other woman.

"Jonah, please," Carly begged. "Please, stop. We can't. Not now."

"Not *now*?" Jonah growled, stilling the sensuous movements of his hands. "When? Tell me when, Silk."

"When I...you..." She put her hands on his shoulders and pushed herself away. "I don't think you should be here."

"Carly, listen to me." Jonah's temper came through in his voice, hoarse whisper though it was. Carly would rather he yelled. "I don't know what Sylvia said to you last week, but I know it was something. You changed after that meeting. It must be something like what she said to me, over and over, about Tory, till I believed it— when it wasn't even close to the truth. Unless you think about it, you probably don't even know what it is."

Carly almost laughed. She knew what it was all right. It was hard to miss a simple declarative statement like *I'm going to have Jonah's baby*.

"It isn't like that," she said.

"Like hell!" Jonah said. "Don't let her do this to us, Carly. Look what I let myself waste with my sister. Years of closeness."

"It won't be years, Jonah," Carly said. "A few days, less than a week. That's not long. Then you'll understand." She pulled out of his arms and tried to step back. Jonah grabbed her, halting her escape. "Until then, I just can't... I'll explain later. It's not that long, Jonah. It will all make sense soon."

He dropped her arm and strode angrily toward the back door. "You've been saying that since I met you, Carly. The only night you were open and honest was the night we met. Then you let your true nature out. Since then, you've had an excuse every time I'm with you why you…'' He spoke in a falsetto, '''Just can't, not yet, Jonah, but any day now.''' He swore. "Forget it, Silk. I can't wait any longer.''

Grabbing his coat off the hook, he stormed out, slamming the door behind him.

Dropping into the recliner by the fire, Carly closed her eyes and tried to let her thoughts flow. If she could just relax, she hoped her exhaustion would let her sleep. But it didn't happen.

For the first time, she knew what Jonah meant. He was right. Without even knowing it, Carly had led him on. She'd pretended she spent time with him for no other reason than their bet—her benevolent wish to show him how wonderful Christmas could be from the giving side. But that was no more true for her than it had been for him.

Jonah at least had been honest about it. *Carly* had kept up her pretense till the end, never admitting that she really wanted him to participate because she loved every minute they spent together.

She had even—she blushed at the admission but didn't hide from it—let him come up tonight because she wanted him to kiss her. She had probably hoped in some unrecognized cell of her brain that he would take her to bed.

But Jonah would never force her. And every time he came close to making love to her, she pushed him away. Her excuses were good, she still believed them. After all, she really *had* promised Sylvia, and even now Carly didn't think Sylvia's request had been unreasonable.

But what if Carly hadn't made that promise to Sylvia? If she'd been free to love Jonah from the beginning, would she have done so? Or would she have found some other excuse to hide because, in fact, she was too scared to take the risk?

Their first night together, everything had felt so safe. She hadn't told Jonah her full name, she hadn't known his. He had recognized long-denied needs in her, but she hadn't had to keep them secret from him. Because she kept herself secret from him instead.

Carly groaned and flipped the recliner back to an upright position. Dear heaven, that was just one more of the many mistakes she'd made with Jonah. As it turned out, she'd kept nothing secret from him, the night hadn't been safe at all, and her needs had turned into love.

But as much as she loved him, she was still hiding. Afraid, just as he said. She told *herself* she trusted him, but she hadn't told him that. She told *herself* she loved him, but she didn't dare tell him that. *She* knew carrying his child filled her with joy, and God only knew what would happen if she told him that.

Most of all, she hadn't ever even hinted that when she found out she was pregnant she had hoped Jonah would want to marry her. Imagining that conversation sent shudders down her spine. Would Jonah laugh at her suggestion? Or just look embarrassed and try to change the subject? Or maybe even deny he was the father, claiming he'd used protection?

Whatever the outcome, the risk of telling him her feelings was so enormous, Carly had never seriously contemplated it.

That's why she had so readily agreed with Sylvia's demand that she wait until after Christmas. Because that, like all the other cowardly maneuvers Carly had used since she met Jonah, was so safe!

Dry-eyed, Carly stared at the temperature gauge on the stove, watching it rise quickly, then slowly fall.

Where was the release of tears when she needed it? But she couldn't cry away her guilt about Jonah.

Tears would just be a cop-out. And she had copped out too often since she'd met him. This time she had to take responsibility for what she was feeling; and for the feelings she hoped she had created in him.

Carly would tell Jonah that she loved him. She would tell him tonight. Just that, nothing more. Just *I love you*. Because she had promised, she would wait to tell him about the baby. But she would tell him tonight that she loved him: *before* she knew how he felt about her, so he would see that for him—and only for him—she would risk her heart.

Wide Spot didn't have many motels to choose from, and Carly picked the nicest one to phone first. "Hunters' Hideaway," a young voice answered on the third ring.

"Good evening," Carly said. "Do you have a Mr. St. John staying there?"

"I think so," said the girl. "Shall I ring that room?"

"Please." Carly listened to the bell, her hope fading with each ring.

Finally the girl came back on the line. "I'm sorry, my dad says they checked out."

"I thought they were going to spend the night," Carly said. "What made them leave? There wasn't an emergency, was there?"

After a pause, a man's voice took the phone. "I don't think there was a problem," he said. "No call came through anyhow. Just up and left, dropped the key at the desk. Paid me for both rooms for the night too. Didn't ask for a refund. Is there a problem?"

"No," Carly sighed. "Thank you."

The fire had gone out in the stove, and, Carly feared one had also gone out in Jonah's heart. Whatever it was

he had felt for her hadn't survived her thoughtless tri-
fling with both their emotions.

As she undressed for bed, she tried to tell herself that
if Jonah really loved her, he wouldn't have given up so
easily. Hank had waited *five years* for Tory. Jonah hadn't
waited two months. But try as she might to blame him,
she knew that the joy he used to show in his eyes when
he saw her had faded this evening. And *she* had caused
that, not Jonah.

Carly was alone again. And, again, she had done it to
herself.

The next two days at the gift shop passed in a frantic
Christmas rush of last-minute buying. Carly never sat
down for a moment. She didn't really get time to eat,
but her stomach wouldn't allow her not to keep something in it. So she ate *biscotti* and Swiss chocolate and
Gouda with English water biscuits.

By evening, when she and DeeDee finally closed the
store, Carly craved real food. But both she and her
mother were too tired to prepare anything, so they settled
for frozen dinners.

After a long bath, Carly flopped on her bed determined to be asleep in five seconds. But her eyes remained stubbornly open. Her body craved rest, but her
mind apparently had no intention of giving it to her. Just
as it had the night before, it obviously meant to keep her
tossing and turning till long after midnight, hashing over
every second of her relationship with Jonah.

Well, tonight Carly wouldn't do it. If she couldn't
sleep, she might as well get up and take action as lie in
bed fretting. The apartment was silent, DeeDee had apparently had no trouble getting to sleep.

Not letting herself hesitate, Carly went to the phone

and punched in Jonah's number. His answering machine picked up, informing callers they'd have a better chance of catching him at work the last two weeks before Christmas.

Carly considered calling Jonah's toy factory, but she didn't have a private number for him at work. No doubt she'd get Sylvia.

She checked her watch, surprised to see it was only a few minutes after eight. Quickly donning loose slacks and a sweater, Carly grabbed her coat and went downstairs.

On the long drive to Bozeman, her subconscious mind let her conscious one know what she was doing. She was going to find Jonah no matter where he was and tell him how much she loved him.

Then—and this scared her far more—she would ask him if he loved her, too. If he said no, she would get back in her car and drive home to Wide Spot and forget she'd ever met him.

Which would be hard to do with his baby growing inside her. But she would manage. Alone.

If Jonah said yes, she would ask him why he hadn't told her before. Why had he left her in this quandary with Sylvia and a baby? If Carly had gone into their last mediation appointment knowing Jonah loved her and wanted to spend the rest of his life with her, she would have felt armed against Sylvia. When Sylvia asked her to wait two weeks or a month...or five years... Carly could have said, "My relationship with Jonah is too serious for that."

Instead Jonah had left her with no real defenses against Sylvia's attack. Without knowing his feelings, Carly's hands were tied. Or at least her tongue was. What did he expect her to do? Tell Sylvia she loved

Jonah too much to stop seeing him when she had no idea whether—

Carly nearly drove off the road as the realization hit her like a wake-up slap. Of *course* that's what Jonah expected. Well, maybe not expected. That's what he wanted. Needed. He needed to know that she really loved him enough to fight for him, no matter how he felt. As far as he knew, Carly had never taken an emotional risk in her life. He probably didn't believe she could.

She thought of the changes Jonah had made since she'd met him. Changes he'd made for her. Look at how much of his December he had spent giving time to other people. Surely a man in the toy business usually devoted this month to work. He must have given every second of his free time to Wide Spot and Carly.

He had even admitted that he'd lost their bet. Though he'd originally let Carly drag him into all her Christmas efforts just as a way to see her, he had participated fully—with an open heart and complete honesty. *That* was why he'd gotten so involved in the programs, because he had done what he'd promised he would do.

It was Carly who had resisted. For every step Jonah took forward, she had taken a step back, away from commitment. But she hadn't actually turned and run. She'd stayed close enough to Jonah to tease him, tantalize him, praying she wouldn't really drive him away. Praying he would make the commitment first, so she could test the idea and see if it was really safe for her cowardly heart.

When she thought about it, she was surprised he'd stayed around as long as he had. For that matter, she was surprised he hadn't dragged her into the backseat of his pickup and...

She shuddered at the thought—shuddered in pleasure.

In fact, the idea sounded so appealing, she wondered if an opportunity for that sort of dragging would occur tonight.

For it seemed unlikely that Jonah would have time to manage that anywhere but a backseat. His business must be operating at its most frantic pace. There seemed slim hope of getting to have a conversation with him at his apartment. And Carly had no intention of having it in his toy factory, where Sylvia could hear every word.

When Carly got to Bozeman, she followed the winding frontage road four miles out of town to the modern-looking building Jonah had once described to her. The parking lot was full, a good indication that Jonah wasn't the only one working late.

Carly drove around the lot, looking for his bright red pickup. When she came to it, she parked and considered her options. She didn't need to walk inside to know she would run into Sylvia. The wide front window had no blinds to hide her view of Sylvia working at a desk.

Carly climbed out of her car, pulling her coat tight. Snow flurries blew stinging flakes against her cheeks. The stars she loved to see remained invisible under the thick cloud cover. But the cold pushed her on with her task.

Relieved to get out of the icy wind, Carly entered Jonah's Toys. "Hi, Sylvia," she said as evenly as she could. "Is Jonah around?"

Sylvia stared at her, wordless for once. "Uh... Of course he is," she said at last. "It's three nights before Christmas, he's as busy as he ever gets. Can I help you?"

"No," Carly said. "I need to see Jonah."

Sylvia's eyes narrowed, her cat's irises glinting suspiciously. "I can get him, I suppose. But I'd better have a good reason before I take him away from the floor. What do you need to see him about?''

Carly had an answer ready. ''Tell him it's about our bet, about the Giving Tree deliveries.''

Sylvia arched her delicate brows. ''Giving Tree?'' she said, making it sound like a disease. ''Surely you don't think Jonah can leave his paying work *now* to help you with some charitable commitment *you* made.''

Much as she wanted to escape this conversation, Carly held her ground. She didn't even look away from Sylvia's irate gaze. ''I just need to talk to him, Sylvia. Do you have a problem with that?''

Sylvia stiffened. Carly had the distinct impression Sylvia wanted to throw her out of the office. But her manners prevented her.

''Certainly I have a problem with it,'' Sylvia said. ''This business is my livelihood, too, as I'm sure you recall from our private conversations.''

''I don't plan to have a four-hour mediation session with him,'' Carly snapped. ''I just need to talk to him for a few minutes about the Giving Tree!''

''What's going on?'' Jonah asked, coming through the door behind Sylvia's desk.

The gaze he turned on Carly did not fill her with ease or comfort. Anger and resentment shone from his dark eyes, taking all hint of sparkle from them. Jonah had always seemed strong, his muscles hard. But until now, Carly had sensed a gentleness in him, at least when it came to her. None of it remained tonight—he was hard from his eyes, to his clenched jaw, to his cold heart.

''What do you want, Carly?'' His voice was cold, as well.

''She wants something *more* for her town's charities,''

Sylvia said as if disgusted by the idea. "As if you hadn't given enough already."

Carly winced, wishing she'd had time to dream up a different excuse to talk to Jonah, one that didn't sound so greedy. "Can we talk somewhere, Jonah?"

"I was just going out for pizza," he said, grabbing his coat from the closet. "I'll walk you to your car."

"You'd better not be gone long, Jonah," Sylvia said. "We need to—"

He cut her off with a gesture. "I've got twenty-five pizzas on order, Sylvia. I won't let them get cold." He opened the door.

As the bitter wind struck her again, Carly wanted to kick herself for not taking advantage of that roaring blaze Jonah had built a few nights ago in her woodstove. They could have had this conversation there: warm, comfortable, a few steps from a bed.

At her car, he spoke before she could open her mouth. "You're here about the Giving Tree presents," he said without asking, his tone sharp with resentment. "I admitted I lost the bet, Carly. Did you think I'd forget?"

"No, Jonah, I—"

"There's a helluva lot I'd like to forget about this season," he went on, "but our bet's not part of it. I didn't lie about that, Carly. *I* don't lie about my emotions."

Carly quit feeling the cold wind, the snow striking her skin. The pain in her heart overcame anything physical. "Jonah—"

"I don't even do business the way I did a few months ago," he went on, his words clipped and furious. "We give away a lot more samples, extra toys to our best customers for nothing, send Christmas gifts to their children. You should be proud of yourself."

"That's wonderful," Carly managed. Her teeth began to chatter. "But—"

"That's what you wanted, right?" The cold didn't seem to be bothering Jonah. His anger must be keeping him warm. "Another convert to your charitable purposes?"

"No, Jonah, I—"

"So if you think I'd forget the Giving Tree, think again."

Carly wondered if he'd noticed that she was trying to say something. If he interrupted her again, she'd punch him. Before she could open her mouth, he jerked open the door to her car.

"*I* remember when I make a commitment." He took her arm and helped her unwillingly into the car. "Now, was there something else, Ms. Underbrook?"

Furious at last, Carly grabbed the door handle, tugging the door free from Jonah's grip. "Yes, *Mr.* St. John, there was. I drove over here in a snowstorm on icy roads to tell you I love you. I love you so much, I couldn't wait another night. When I'm around you, my heart feels like it will explode from all the love I feel—it hasn't been good for anything but loving you since the moment we met. I never even knew what love was before. And I know I'll never feel this way again. No one could feel this way twice in one lifetime."

"Silk!" Jonah's voice cracked.

"But I guess you don't have time to listen to that or your damn pizzas will get cold," she continued, warming to her subject. "Don't worry, I won't take another second of your precious time. Better hurry back to Sylvia before she calls out the cavalry." Carly slammed her door.

"Carly," Jonah shouted. "Wait!"

Carly turned the ignition and drove off, leaving Jonah standing in the lot staring after her, his unfastened coat flapping in the wind.

CHAPTER TEN

THE following night, Carly tugged on her Santa's elf suit, with more anticipation than her usual joy in this evening could explain. For she knew that Jonah would be here soon. His insistence that *he* never forgot a commitment made her positive he would come.

Of course, he could just send a messenger with the toys, but if he'd meant to do that, surely the toys would have arrived today during normal working hours. No, Carly fully expected to see him any minute.

If she hadn't been quite positive Jonah meant to come tonight, she wouldn't have driven off last night in a snit. Oh, maybe she'd still have slammed the door in his face and started her motor, maybe even backed out of the parking space. But when he called out to her, she'd have relented.

At least that's what she decided on the way home. She'd gotten so annoyed by his holier than thou lecture to her—which probably wouldn't have infuriated her quite so much if the temperature had been above zero and the snow hadn't kept hitting her in the face—and by his assumption that she had only come for more handouts, that she'd really enjoyed the gesture of leaving him in the parking lot.

But if she'd thought for one second that she wouldn't see him again in twenty-four hours, she'd have followed him to the pizza parlor and had it out with him there. The pizzas wouldn't have gotten back to Jonah's Toys a little cooled off—they'd have congealed.

She twisted, trying to pull up the zipper on the back of her velour suit. "Mom," she finally called. "Can you help me with this zipper?"

She glared at her reflection in the mirror, turning sideways. She simply hadn't gained that much weight, a few pounds perhaps. Not that *she* couldn't feel the difference. Jeans had grown increasingly uncomfortable. But she didn't believe it was visible to the casual observer.

"Help with your zipper?" Jonah said, walking into her bedroom without knocking. "I thought you'd never ask."

Carly shrieked and turned her exposed back away from him, then felt silly. He'd certainly seen more than her back that night in Bozeman.

"Where's Mom?"

"She decided to spend the evening with her fiancé," Jonah said. "And before you ask, yes, I banished her. Tommy lent me his Santa suit. I'm delivering toys with you." He grinned that devilish grin that made her shiver. "Then I'm going to deliver something else *to* you."

"Jonah, I love you," Carly said, walking toward him. "I do. I love you so much."

Jonah closed his eyes as a series of powerful emotions crossed his face. He grabbed her and hauled her close. "I love you, too, Silk. But I'd begun to think I'd never hear you say the words."

"You never told me," she murmured, reveling in the feel of snuggling against his chest.

"No," Jonah said. "I couldn't. I needed to know…if I really meant anything to you. I was afraid I'd spend the rest of my life wondering if you just ended up with me because I was safe. Or if you really loved me as much as I love you."

"Oh, Jonah," Carly said. "I'm sorry it took me so

long to figure that out. All our time together was so wonderful, I just enjoyed it and didn't ever think about...well, about what it was doing to you.'' She nestled closer into his chest, pressing her lips to his throat, kissing and nibbling. "Will you ever forgive me?"

"You bet," he said. He chuckled, then let it turn into a laugh. "I forgave you last night when I watched you drive off, leaving me in that cursed blizzard. Freezing my ass and too damn busy to even consider driving after you." He leaned down and chewed her earlobe. "Want to know what I thought of all night long?"

"Me, too." Carly quivered at his touch. "I feel like such a fool. I wasted so much time."

"It was a messy situation," Jonah said. "Still is, I guess. Have you said anything to Sylvia?"

"No, I..." Carly felt as if he'd poured ice water over her. "Have you?"

He shook his head. "I thought I'd wait till we got all our Christmas orders out." He shrugged. "The business means more to her than anything else. Besides, I wanted to see you first."

"Well," Carly said, her desire cooled for the moment, "we'd better get these presents ready to deliver."

"Are you going like that?" Jonah asked, his grin back in place. "Or shall I zip you up?"

Carly made a face at him and turned her back. Jonah slid his warm hands over her bare back, down to the base of her spine where the zipper was stuck. It was only with a major effort at resistance that she kept herself from turning around and throwing herself into his arms.

Jonah made a pretense of struggling mightily with the zipper. "This the same suit you wore at Thanksgiving, Silk?"

"Mmm-hmm," Carly murmured, barely aware of what he was asking.

"I knew it was tight." He pulled the zipper up and leaned forward to whisper against her neck. "I mean, every man at the party knew that. But I never realized it was *this* tight." He turned her to face him. "Christmas cookies?"

Carly's cheeks throbbed with heat. She *still* felt constrained from telling him about the baby. "Funny." She twisted out of his arms. "We'd better—"

Jonah stepped in front of her. "Hey, Silk, what's the matter? I'm only teasing." He put his hands on her shoulders and slid them down to her hands, softly massaging the palms. "I love every inch of your body. Eat all the cookies you want."

She shook her head, trying not to melt into his ministering touch. "It's not that. I just…we need to get this done. Then we can think about all that other stuff."

"Damn it!" Jonah growled, a deep frown creasing the skin between his brows. "What's bothering you?" He grabbed her upper arms. "Don't do this to us anymore, Silk. Ever." His dark gaze looked so intense it seemed he could see into her soul. "You've got to trust me. As long as you live, don't ever make me wait to know how you feel about something. Understand? You can say anything to me. There is absolutely nothing about you, about your feelings, your thoughts, that I don't want to hear."

"Jonah, I do trust you, I do." Carly looked around the small room, wishing there was a place in it she could hide from this conversation. "And I want to tell you everything about me, to find out everything about you. But I…there's just this one other thing."

His brows dropped lower. "What the hell did Sylvia say to you last week? Tell me!"

Carly felt tears sting her eyes. She swallowed. "I can't."

Jonah grabbed her upper arms and brought her face close to his. Carly could see he had every intention of erupting into the tongue-lashing of the century. But she could also see his lips, his jaw, his wonderful dark eyes, all those parts of his handsome face that had made her gasp with pleasure during their first dance together.

She gasped again now. This beautiful man loved her. She could hardly believe it. Even more mind-boggling was how much she loved him.

She couldn't help it. Even against the pressure of his hands holding her back, she raised her lips to his and kissed him with all the love consuming her. Jonah couldn't resist, he groaned as he moved his hands to her back and pulled her tight. He, too, must feel overwhelmed by love.

His hands covered her breasts with new demand, yet new gentleness. Carly's nipples peaked in his fingers, and her breasts felt achy and heavy. Whimpering with want, she slid between his thighs and wrapped her arms behind his waist.

"Jonah, I...love you," she said, fighting to breathe in enough air to speak. "I want to tell you everything. And I will. Just not tonight."

"If you think you can distract me this way every time I'm ticked off—" Jonah grinned a crooked grin "—you're right." He pulled in a long breath and let it gust from his lungs. "I'll let it rest for tonight. Tomorrow morning at ten, Sylvia and I will be in your office for our final mediation appointment. Then I'm going to find out everything that's going on."

At the thought of not having to dissemble anymore

around Jonah, Carly felt an overwhelming relief. "Will you…um, drive over together?" she asked.

"Now what difference does that make?" Jonah asked.

"Well, I thought, you know, if you were in different cars," Carly said, "you could stay afterward and…"

"And…?" Jonah smiled, his eyes warming at her words. "I think you'll be too tired by then, Silk. I plan to stay tonight."

"Really, Jonah?" Carly couldn't help the sigh of longing that escaped her before reality intruded again. "Mom will be home before we get done with these presents and…well, she and Tommy have always been careful around me. I don't know if it would be fair to…"

Jonah sighed. "That's a problem." He lifted his shoulders in a shrug, though a grimace ridged his brow. "What's one more night, I guess."

"Right." Carly felt the ache of unsatisfied desire and sympathized with Jonah's frustration. "And we have so many deliveries to make this year, we may be too tired to be in the mood by the time we're done."

Jonah shook his head. "Trust me, Silk, I'll be in the mood." At her remonstrating look, he jammed his fists into his pockets. "Okay, okay, how many deliveries do we have to make?"

"Well, not enough really. There were three cards that no one took."

"I got them," Jonah said.

"You got them?" Carly asked. "What do you mean?"

"I took those cards and bought the presents," Jonah replied. "I also brought dolls and video games for all the other kids." He flicked up a brow. "Did I forget something?"

"You are just wonderful," she said.

He took her face between his hands. "It took you long enough to figure that out."

"I figured it out right away," Carly said. "That's what scared me so much."

"Just don't forget it." Jonah turned her toward the door to her bedroom and slapped her behind. "Now let's get going before we get distracted again."

Next morning, Carly deserted DeeDee at the gift shop on their busiest day to go back to her mediation office. If her defection bothered her mother, she didn't say anything.

Carly turned up the heat and made coffee, feeling much more assured than she had the last two times she'd readied this office for an appointment. Not that she could really call herself relaxed. The fact that she'd nibbled away two plates of homemade Christmas cookies was clear evidence of her nerves.

But at least today, in any disputes that might develop, Carly knew Jonah would stand one hundred percent on her side.

Disputes *might* develop? Carly dropped a scoopful of coffee grounds. How on earth could a dispute not develop when one man and two women, one pregnant and one wanting to be with his babies, all sat down in the same room to hash things out? She leaned down to sweep up the spilled grounds, and her stomach lurched from the pressure of her belt.

Oh, Lord, it was going to feel good to admit her condition and be able to wear clothes that accommodated her insides enough to release her from this constant queasiness.

Sylvia knocked but didn't wait for Carly to open the door. She walked in and began hanging up her coat.

"Jonah's not here yet?" she asked, walking toward the chair she always took.

"No," Carly said, wishing with all her heart he were.

"Did you leave at the same time?"

"Actually he left a few minutes before me," Sylvia said, folding her hands and crossing her ankles. "But he had a delivery to drop off on the way."

Perspiration beaded on Carly's scalp. Sylvia's movements exactly mirrored her movements on every other visit to Carly's office. Obviously Jonah hadn't told her anything. She was far too calm and controlled.

"Do you know why Jonah made this appointment this morning?" Sylvia asked.

Oh, where was Jonah? Carly wondered. "Um, he wanted to discuss the problems—"

"I know what he wants to discuss," Sylvia said. "I just wonder why he suddenly decided we had to settle things smack in the middle of the Christmas rush."

"I guess he didn't want to leave things in the air over the holiday," Carly said. "Probably wanted everything decided so he could enjoy Christmas."

"Enjoy Christmas?" Sylvia said, rolling her eyes. "I don't see how we'll manage that. He informed me yesterday, we're going to his family's ranch for two days. You can't imagine how cluttered and noisy that place is. I think it would be far better for us, with the special gift I have in mind, to have a quiet Christmas at home. Don't you agree? Maybe you could tell Jonah that, too."

Carly just stared, a dreadful thought forming in her mind. She did not believe Jonah had left her last night and gone home to Sylvia's to discuss where they would spend Christmas. Yet Sylvia had delivered that last little speech with such believable casualness, if Carly hadn't seen Jonah last night, she would have believed her.

But if this was a lie, what other lies had Sylvia told? Especially—

Before she could complete the thought, Jonah entered the office. As he hung his sheepskin jacket on a coat hook, Carly let her gaze run over his muscular chest, clearly visible under the turtleneck and sweater he wore. Her eyes roamed lower, admiring those delicious parts of him covered by his blue jeans.

The man was so beautiful, his heart so warm and generous, she couldn't blame Sylvia for not wanting to lose him. But if what Jonah said was true, Sylvia only cared about the money she would lose. Carly could hardly believe it, not after the things Sylvia had said to her.

Jonah met Carly's longing gaze, and his eyes filled with love and heat, reminding her forcefully of their last kiss on the narrow back steps of her apartment. He'd refused to come up, swearing if he did, he wouldn't leave.

But the kiss had deepened and lengthened, till Carly didn't even remain on her feet. Pressed between Jonah and the wall, she felt herself gradually being lifted on his knee. Her moans grew loud and frantic. Clinging to him, kissing him everywhere her lips could reach, she begged him to come upstairs with her.

Jonah clutched her hard, immobilizing her against him. When his breathing had calmed, he said, "DeeDee's home, Silk."

Shuddering, Carly continued to hold on to him, until she thought her knees could walk her all the way up the stairs. At her door, she looked back down at him. "I love you," she whispered.

"Go to bed," Jonah said, "and think of me." He let his lips curl into that incredibly suggestive grin. "Which means you won't sleep a wink. I better see big dark circles under your eyes come morning.''

Carly wished he'd arrived before Sylvia, so he could come closer and see if her eyes looked sleepy enough to satisfy him.

Instead Jonah looked back and forth between the two women. ''Something going on already? You both look a little…tense.''

''Not I, Jonah,'' Sylvia said. ''You sounded so final this morning, I assume you've figured out a way to settle our differences.''

''No, Sylvia,'' Jonah said. ''I haven't even thought about the business.''

Sylvia returned her coffee mug to the table with such a smack Carly expected it to shatter. ''Really?'' Sylvia's brows rose nearly to her perfectly coiffed bangs. ''Then what in the name of heaven did you make us drive all the way over here for…today of all days?''

Jonah answered without even glancing at Carly. He must have figured out that Carly had no idea how to answer Sylvia's questions, and he would have to. ''I want to know what you said to Carly last week, Sylvia.''

''I *beg* your pardon,'' Sylvia said. ''I believe that conversation was confidential.'' She shot her tawny gaze at Carly. ''Didn't you make that commitment to me? Or did I misunderstand? Was there some fine print at the end of your promise that I failed to read?''

''No, Sylvia,'' Carly said. ''No fine print. I kept my word, and I will continue to. But Jonah didn't want to wait any longer.'' Lowering her voice, she fluttered her hand between them. ''You know…you said you wanted to tell him Christmas morning. That's only one more day. What can it hurt? He's very impatient.''

"No need to whisper," Sylvia said. "I don't plan to say a word until I think it's right…for *me*."

Jonah stood and walked around the table to Sylvia's chair. He stood over her, making her tip her head back to see him. "Sylvia." He didn't raise his voice, but if he had used that tone with Carly, she'd have cringed. "I'm in love with Carly, I want to marry her, have babies with her. I won't change my mind. If you want the damn business bad enough, I won't even fight that. You can have it, I'll go start another one somewhere else."

"I have no intention of giving you up as a business partner," Sylvia said. "I want half of the business *we* make together." Her voice turned shrill. "It won't last without you, and you know it. What will I do then?"

Carly felt her jaw flop open in surprise. Jonah had been right all along. For all Sylvia's threats, she'd never really wanted to break up the business. She'd just been looking for ways to keep Jonah in it.

Jonah leaned down and put his hands on the arms of her chair, trapping her in her seat. "Sylvia, focus on what this meeting is about. I don't give a damn about the business. You can stay in it, sell it, keep it, whatever the hell you want. What *I* want is Carly. And I want her disengaged entirely from this nonsense between us. Now tell me what you told her last week, or I'll fight you every step of the way in court. Even if you win, you'll get nothing, because you'll have to use all your assets on legal fees."

"Are you threatening me?" Sylvia asked, her tone admirably strong, Carly thought.

"You're damn right," Jonah said. "Nothing or something, which do you want?" He grabbed her chin and tipped her eyes up to him. "Remember, I can go start another toy store—I'm the one who makes the toys. You get this one or nothing. Decide now, it's your last chance.''

Sylvia put a hand on Jonah's chest and pushed him up to a standing position. ''Tell me, darling,'' she said. Though she tried for the disinterested tone she affected so well, Carly heard a new tenseness in the other woman's voice. ''Does your offer to buy me out still stand?''

''Yes, fine, whatever,'' Jonah said impatiently. ''Now what the hell did you—''

Sylvia waved him to silence and turned to regard Carly with utter disdain. ''Honestly, you fool,'' she said. ''Did you really think I would allow myself to get in that disgusting condition? Believe me, I will *never*—'' she shuddered ''—let that happen to me. And if I did, I'd take care of it as soon as I discovered it.'' She let out a snort of a laugh, expressing disgust for everything and everyone within her hearing. ''A baby. It's beyond me how you could believe that.''

''A *what*?!'' Jonah roared.

Carly's cheeks burned with humiliation. She wanted to slide under the table and never have to look Jonah in the eye. It seemed so obvious now that Sylvia had been lying. How could she ever have believed that Jonah had betrayed her? In fact, by believing Sylvia for even a second, Carly had betrayed Jonah. How could he ever forgive her?

Sylvia rose and pushed past Jonah, who stood staring at her, his mouth agape. ''Good luck with your 'little woman,' Jonah. She's cute, but awfully gullible.''

Jonah grabbed Sylvia's arm as she reached for her coat. ''You told her that I had gotten you pregnant?''

Sylvia regarded Jonah's hand on her arm the way

she'd look at bird droppings that had landed on her, then lifted her gaze to his face. He didn't release her.

"Answer me, Sylvia," he said coldly.

"No indeed, darling. I just dropped a few hints," Sylvia said, her tone sticky with false sweetness. "And she, your own true love, believed the worst. Surely you told her we hadn't engaged in that sort of thing for years? Well, she didn't believe you, dear, she believed *me*."

Jonah dropped his hand. Sylvia took her coat off the hook, slipped her arms into the sleeves and began very deliberately fastening the buttons.

Jonah stood between Carly and Sylvia, not moving. Carly's stomach knotted and lurched in waves. She longed for the moment Sylvia would leave her office. And she feared it with a dread that made her heart beat painfully in her chest.

Jonah was furious. She could feel it just looking at his back. She didn't even blame him. Sylvia's barbs had hit their mark too well: Carly had put more faith in Sylvia's lies than Jonah's love.

In a moment, he was going to turn and look at Carly. She already knew what she would see in his expression. Disappointment, anger, disbelief. And profound hurt. She only prayed that she wouldn't also see what she feared the most: his rejection. His farewell.

What could Carly say to him to make him change his mind? How could she make him understand why she'd believed Sylvia? At the moment, she didn't understand herself.

At the door, Sylvia put her gloved hand on Jonah's cheek. "It's been an exciting ride, my sweet."

Jonah didn't even bother to shake off her hand. "Get

out, Sylvia. I'll have my lawyer send you the papers to sign. Don't ever let me see you at Jonah's Toys again.''

Jonah shut the door behind her and his shoulders slumped. He leaned his head against the jamb, saying nothing.

"Jonah," Carly said, wishing fear didn't make her voice so tight. "We have to talk about this."

Without turning, Jonah pulled his jacket off the hook. "I don't think I want to talk about it now, Carly." Oh, how she wished he'd call her Silk.

He reached for the doorknob and walked out. Carly stared at the closed door, assuring herself that he would be back. She wished she believed her assurances.

She started calmly toward the door, then ran, tripping over the chairs and barking her shin. She squealed and swore and grabbed the doorknob, just as Jonah jerked the door open from the other side.

Carly flew outside into the parking lot, stumbling over the curb and landing on her backside on a pile of shoveled snow. Jonah was beside her in an instant.

"Sorry," he said, not quite meeting her eyes. His mouth twitched. Then he chuckled. Then he laughed heartily. "God, Silk, are you always going to find a way to deflect my anger so effectively? Though, given a choice—" he wobbled a palm back and forth "—I like last night's methods better than this slapstick."

"Slapstick!" Carly said, as the ache in her backside subsided. "*You're* the one who threw me into the snowbank."

"We can argue that one later." Jonah let out a disgusted breath as he reached for her hand and pulled her to her feet. Turning her around, he dusted the snow off her with enough enthusiasm to make her sure he enjoyed the task more than she. "I came back to give you the

lecture of a lifetime, till you were damn sorry you'd
made such a mistake about me. Instead you make me
laugh.''

"Oh, Jonah," Carly said. "Don't you know how
sorry I am already? Nothing you can say would make it
any worse." She shook her head. "No, that's not true.
You could make it worse if you tell me you don't love
me anymore."

Jonah stuffed his fists into his sheepskin pockets.
"When I stormed out of your office just now, I thought
that's what I should say." He frowned and sat down on
the bumper of his pickup. "God*damn* it, Silk, how the
hell could you think that about me?"

CHAPTER ELEVEN

CARLY bit her lip, holding back tears. Boy, would she be glad when she got her emotions back under her control. She wondered what month that happened, or would she be this way till the baby was born. She swallowed hard, remembering there was that still to tell Jonah, too: about their baby. But it didn't seem exactly the way to start this discussion.

"J-J-Jonah," she began, her teeth chattering.

Seeming suddenly to recognize that Carly was cold, Jonah took off his coat and held it out for her. Gratefully she stuck her arms into sleeves that hung inches below her hands. His heat still warmed the coat, and his musky male scent surrounded her.

Jonah pulled the coat tight around her, then tugged her by the lapels toward the door to her office. With his hand on the doorknob, he stopped frowning.

"Reminds me too much of Sylvia in there," he grumbled.

Grabbing a windbreaker from behind the seat in his pickup, Jonah put his arm around Carly's shoulders and started walking down Main Street. At the café, he held the door for her.

"Think you can behave yourself in public?" he asked sarcastically.

Carly entered the restaurant and went straight to the booth in the back corner by the pellet stove. Sitting by its heat, watching the flames dance, she began to relax. Jonah sat on the bench on the other side of the table, making sure she knew he hadn't forgiven her yet. But at least he was here, with her, willing to listen.

After he told the waitress they only wanted coffee, he leaned back against the seat, looking like a judge waiting to hear the evidence.

Carly didn't speak till the heat and coffee had made her teeth quit chattering. "Jonah, you kept telling me not to worry about what happened to your business."

Jonah sipped coffee and said nothing.

"But I never quite believed that," Carly went on, "because of the other things you said when I first met you. About how you didn't want to lose the business you'd built up that had your name on it. And you didn't want to spend years in court, fighting over it."

Jonah looked at her with no smile on his lips or in his eyes. "I never said anything like that after I fell in love with you."

"But *I* didn't know that," Carly said. "Was it really so unreasonable of me to believe that helping you keep your business was something you really wanted?"

"I guess not." His tone reflected suspicion, as if he hated to concede anything at this point.

"And Sylvia reminded me of that whenever she could, telling me you wouldn't thank me if you had to get a lawyer, things like that." Carly held up a hand when he started to object. "And since I thought she was right, Jonah, that made me believe she cared about you."

Jonah shook his head. "I told you again and again that all Sylvia cared about was how much money *she* took out of the business."

"I know," Carly sighed. "And *that* I should have believed. But Sylvia didn't ever talk that way. And you *had* loved her enough once to ask her to marry you, and she'd accepted. I had to believe that she loved you, or at least had loved you then.''

''She probably did,'' Jonah said impatiently. ''As much as Sylvia could. But what does that have to do with *us*?''

Carly wanted to move around the table and sit closer to Jonah when she said these things, but he didn't look receptive. ''Jonah, I know how much you want a child. Sylvia knows that, too, knows what it would do to you to hear she was willing to have your baby. Even this morning, when she said that about a baby, you jumped, like someone had hit you.''

''Yeah.'' Jonah nodded. ''For less than a second, I got a rush of...whatever. Joy, I guess. I didn't believe it long enough to figure out the emotion. And of course I knew instantly, even if it were true, it wasn't *my* baby.''

Hoping he was softening, Carly covered Jonah's hand, clenched into a fist on the table. He didn't relax, but he didn't pull his hand away, either.

''I couldn't believe that anyone who had ever loved you, who knew how much you wanted children, could possibly lie about having your baby. It would be so cruel...beyond cruel.'' She looked into his eyes. ''I love you too much to even consider...it just...never crossed my mind that she would be willing to hurt you that way. She said she loves you!'' Carly covered her face with her hands.

Silence fell while Jonah thought over Carly's words. She kept her hands over her face, afraid to watch the play of emotion on his. She heard him let a long breath from his lungs, felt his hand lightly touch her wrist, slide slowly down her arm. Lowering her hands, her face a grimace of hope and fear, Carly met his eyes.

He was smiling. Not that broad, eye-crinkling smile

she had come to love. But a smile nevertheless. He held out his hand palm up and when she took it, he tugged gently. "C'mere," he said huskily.

Carly moved around the table so fast she nearly kicked over a couple of chairs. "Oh, Jonah," she said, snuggling into the back corner of the booth with him. "Jonah, I love you so much."

He held her against him, stroking her hair. "I've been mad at you for weeks for acting *un*trusting, I guess I can forgive you for being too trusting once." He shook his head. "You sure picked the wrong time, though."

"I know," Carly said. "Believe me, I know it better than you."

Jonah kissed the top of her head. Even that brotherly sort of kiss made Carly wish they'd had this discussion in her apartment instead of such a public place. She wished it so much, she could barely concentrate on his words.

"What do you mean, 'better than me,' Carly?"

Carly drew back far enough to look him in the eyes. She needed to see if the golden flecks had come back or if his uncertainty about her love still made his eyes solidly dark brown. Tipping her head, she studied him. Very very dark, but just a tiny flicker of golden softness.

"Jonah," she said. "I know you want to have a baby sometime. Probably sometime soon, right?"

The gold flecks grew warmer. "Yeah," he said. "The sooner the better." He touched her cheek. "But not until you're ready. All the way ready." His crooked grin turned up one side of his mouth. "It's not something I plan to do on my own, Silk."

There, he'd called her "Silk." It was safe now. "Well, I was just thinking..." Carly kissed his mouth, on one side, then the other, then in the middle. She leaned up close to him so she could speak into his ear. "Nine months is *such* a long time. Do you really want to wait that long?"

Jonah grabbed her shoulders and held her away from him. His eyes narrowed. "What in the hell are you talking about?"

She watched his eyes as she spoke. "How does seven-and-a-half months sound?"

As Carly watched Jonah's expression change from hope and disbelief to joy and love, she knew that all her life she would treasure this moment. All her life she would be grateful he had held her where she could see his face when he heard her words.

Jonah put his hand on her belly and smiled. "Not Christmas cookies?"

"Not," she agreed.

He kept looking at her, not moving his hand, as a frown gradually came over his face. She didn't need to hear him tell her what troubled him now.

"I didn't tell you because, well, I didn't know right away," Carly said. "I mean, I thought you used..."

"I did," Jonah said.

"So when I started all this crying and nausea, I didn't figure it out at first." Carly sighed as Jonah sat up straight to listen to her. "I just found out—that day I saw you at the discount store. I didn't know till after I saw you."

"That was two weeks ago, Carly." Jonah sounded hurt. Carly wished again they were somewhere she could kiss him. "My God, weren't you even going to give me a chance? This is *my* child, too. You couldn't possibly think I didn't want to raise him."

Carly frowned. "Her."

Jonah rolled his eyes, but a bit of the tenseness left

his mouth. "Your ability to change the subject at the wrong time is Olympian."

"I was going to tell you, Jonah," Carly said, stroking a palm down his stubbly cheek. "I tried to call you that night. Then the next day I met with Sylvia and found out *she* wanted your baby and might already be—"

"So you put your needs after hers," Jonah said grimly.

Carly nodded. "I guess that's such a habit with me, I kind of…"

"You kind of," Jonah said sarcastically, "forgot about *my* needs."

Carly winced. "Not really. I mean…well, I did wonder how many babies you'd really want to have at once. And if…"

"You weren't even going to tell me, were you, Silk?"

Silk, that was such a giveaway. "Of course I was going to tell you. Sometime."

Jonah took her upper arms and brought her face close to his. "If you weren't pregnant, so help me, I'd turn you over my knee."

"I guess if we're going to stay together," she said, giggling, "I'll have to get pregnant a lot." She gave him a grin. "You know how I like to feel safe."

Jonah shook his head, but he was smiling now, too. "You won't be able to stay pregnant *that* much, so you'll have to clean up your act instead."

Carly held up her right hand. "I swear I'll never again mediate a dispute between you and a former lover."

"That's something, but not enough." He stroked a finger along her jaw, curling it under her chin to lift her gaze to his. "Tell me why you're going to marry me this afternoon?"

"This afternoon?" Carly cried, then lowered her

voice, wondering if everyone in the restaurant knew exactly what they were saying over in this corner. "Because I love you!"

"And?"

Carly looked at the expectant, hopeful look in Jonah's eyes. "Because I need you, Jonah. I need you because I love you so much. I needed you the moment I met you, that's why I seduced you at the party. Now I need you even more because I love you more. And our baby needs you, too."

Suddenly Jonah seemed as eager to leave the restaurant as Carly. Sliding her off the bench seat, he threw a couple of dollars on the table, and grabbed their coats. She was still trying to get hers buttoned when they stepped onto the sidewalk.

Though they stood in front of the café window, all the restraint Jonah had felt in the restaurant seemed to evaporate. Grabbing Carly around the waist, he lifted her into the air and spun her around and around, shouting with joy.

When her head whirled, he put her down, pulled her close into his body and brought his mouth to hers. One hand cupped the back of her head, while the other moved beneath the lapels of his too big coat and massaged down her belly till his big palm covered her womb. Moans came from her throat as his tongue traced the curve of the roof of her mouth and his hand traced the curves of her slightly swelling body.

When Jonah finally lifted his head, they heard muffled applause and laughter from inside the café. Blushing, Carly glanced through the window and saw what looked like half the population of Wide Spot giving them grins and thumbs-ups. Jonah gave them all a salute and started down the street.

He leaned down to whisper in her ear. "I need you, too, Silk, and love you more than I'll ever be able to tell you." He stopped and held her. "You know that, don't you? I want this baby, but not as much as I want you." He cupped her cheek and that devilish glint came into his eyes. "It's because he's *our* baby that I want him so much."

"Jonah," Carly said as seriously as she could, "I hate to disappoint you, but I've already decided this baby is a girl."

"And when did you decide that?"

"Oh, about the moment I thought you were sleeping with Sylvia."

Jonah rolled his eyes, grinning. "I don't think I want to hear that train of thought." He placed a light kiss on her lips and started walking again. "Tell me what you thought when you first found out."

"By the time I saw the spot turning pink," Carly said, "I'd already driven all the way to Bozeman and back thinking about it. Knowing it for sure just filled me with joy."

Jonah sighed. "I wish I'd been there."

"Me, too," Carly said. "But you will be next time."

"Damn right." Jonah opened the door to his pickup and put a hand under her elbow to help her up.

Carly started to climb in when she realized she had no idea where they were going. As she turned to ask him, DeeDee came out the back door of the shop.

"Carly," she said. "Are you going to work at all today or shall I see if I can get someone else?"

Jonah answered DeeDee's question and Carly's unasked one at the same time. "Sorry, she won't be back. We're going to Idaho, it's the fastest place to get married.'' He grabbed his future mother-in-law and gave her a hug. ''Thanks for your blessing, *Gramma*.''

The quick burst of surprise on DeeDee's face was instantly replaced with a broad smile. ''Gramma?'' she said happily. ''Thank heavens that's it. I was beginning to think I'd never be able to keep enough *biscotti* in the store.'' She hugged Carly, giving her a big kiss. ''Good luck, darling. You can be my matron of honor on New Year's.''

Carly smiled and waited until DeeDee had retreated inside out of the cold before she said, ''Can't I grab a few—''

''Nope,'' Jonah said. ''You won't have anything on for most of this trip, and we'll be back tomorrow.'' He took her elbow again and lifted her into the truck.

A sigh of pleasure with a hint of exasperation left her as she landed on the seat. In her heart she was deliriously happy that the man she loved wouldn't let her out of his sight long enough to pack an overnight bag. She waited until he'd turned onto the highway to tease him.

''I suppose that was your idea of a proposal?''

Jonah shifted into a lower gear to drive up the hill outside of town. ''What kind of a question is that?''

''You said not to hide my needs from you.'' Carly put her hand on his thigh. ''I guess I need you to ask me, Jonah.''

Jonah slowed the truck and pulled onto the side of the road. Taking Carly's hand, he brought it to his lips. ''It's too cramped in here to get down on one knee, Silk. But if you think I'm taking your acceptance for granted, think again. I didn't ask because I'm afraid to give you the chance to say no.''

Carly clutched his hand, squeezing his fingers till she thought she'd break them. ''Oh dear Lord, Jonah, nothing on this earth could make me say anything but yes to you about anything.''

Jonah smiled, his hint of devilishness flaring. ''Good, love, because after you promise to love me forever, marry me and take my name, I have another question for you.''

Carly giggled. ''That is *so* sneaky.''

''Just answer, Silk.'' Jonah kissed her lips. ''You demanded this proposal, now quit dancing around and answer me.''

''You know the answer is yes.'' Carly leaned against his shoulder.

''Good girl,'' Jonah said. ''Yes to all of that?''

''Yes, yes, and yes.''

''That's what I like to hear from my woman,'' Jonah said. He shifted into gear and drove up the mountain.

He remained silent as he drove over the pass, making Carly wonder if he was concentrating on the icy roads or thinking something over.

When they had driven another twenty miles, he finally said, ''Now that I have you captive far from home, I can tell you what I'm giving you for a wedding present.'' He shot her a quick look. ''The day we get back, I'm paying all your father's debts.''

''Oh, no, you're not,'' Carly said, sitting up straight. ''They're not your obligation, Jonah. You don't have to do that.''

''They're not your obligation, either, Silk,'' Jonah said. ''But you won't ever feel free of worry till they're paid. I used to think it was silly that you were even bothering, but I realize now that you need to do this.''

''You're right,'' Carly said. ''I guess for the last five years, that's the only need I could express.''

"I understand that," Jonah said. He pulled the truck off the road again.

"We're never going to get to Idaho," Carly said, "if you stop every few miles."

"Don't joke now, Carly," Jonah said, "this is serious."

She nodded. "I won't change my mind, Jonah."

"Those debts are not a moral obligation of yours, Silk, they're not *your* debts." He turned up a palm. "So it's just money. I have it, I want to give it to you. And your mother."

"But…" Carly was having trouble arguing because the picture he made her see was so enticing. To be able to take money she and her mother earned and spend it on themselves, maybe on the layette for her baby… A wedding gift for Jonah. She shuddered with pleasure at the idea. But *Jonah* hadn't taken on this obligation.

"Silk, did you think I was kidding about our bet?" Jonah asked. "About how much I liked thinking of Christmas as a season of giving instead of just a profitable season for my business?"

"No, I didn't," Carly said. "The way you acted with Mrs. Watson, I could tell you meant it."

He pulled her onto his lap and kissed her. "I like Mrs. Watson, I like Annie, I like all your friends. But you are the only person in the world I love this way. I feel like I'll strangle if I can't tell you every few minutes, and I'll lose my mind if I can't make love to you every night."

Carly felt her bones dissolving as she melted against him. "Does this have something to do with giving?"

"I want to give something to you, too, Carly, the gift of freedom from worry." He kissed one of her eyes. "I'm glad to give it to DeeDee, too. But it's you, the woman I love, I want to give to the most.'' He kissed her other eye. ''And I've never given you anything. Please let me give you this. Let me give it to you and give it to us.''

''Oh, Jonah!'' Carly said. ''Never given me anything? You've given me my heart back, you've given me back a reason for living, you've given me *everything*.''

''And now I'm giving you this, paying your debts.'' He cupped her cheeks. ''Say yes.''

''It sounds so tacky compared to all that other stuff,'' Carly said. ''But…yes.'' She took a big breath, realizing she could accept this gift from Jonah and from no one else because she knew it came only from love. ''Thank you, Jonah.''

''Thank you, Carly,'' he said. ''Now…'' His grin was back. ''…Shall we climb into the back? Or continue eloping?''

''Oh, what a choice.'' Carly giggled. ''I think we should climb into the back.''

Jonah shook his head in mock dismay. ''You are *so* naughty, I noticed that the night I met you.'' He slid her onto the seat. ''We'll finish eloping, then we'll climb into a motel.'' He regarded her sternly. ''Say, 'Yes, Jonah.'''

''Yes, Jonah.'' She ran her finger over his full bottom lip. ''All these yeses are *your* wedding gift. You know better than to expect this treatment regularly, don't you?''

He looked at the truck ceiling. ''Maybe I should try for a few 'yessirs' while you're in this mood.''

''Don't press your luck.''

He laughed. ''Want to make another bet that you'll say it before the day is out?''

''Not a chance.''

"Try this. If you say, 'Yessir, Jonah,' I'll kiss you again before we head for Idaho."

"Oh, you sneaky, underhanded..." Carly looked at his slightly open mouth and capitulated completely. "Yessir, Jonah, please kiss me again." As his lips came toward hers, she knew and she admitted, "You made me trust you, Jonah. I never thought I would trust any man again. And I know you'd never really make me say that to mean it. So I'll always say it for a kiss." She put her hand behind his neck and tugged. "Now kiss me."

"Yes, ma'am."

Jonah kissed her till the only thought she could keep in her head was how much she loved him. Then he started the truck and drove toward their wedding.

Fill your holiday with...
excitement, magic and love!

Mistletoe Kisses

December is the time for Christmas carols, surprises
wrapped in colored paper and kisses under the mistletoe.
Mistletoe Kisses is a festive collection of stories about three
humbug bachelors and the feisty heroines who entice them
to ring in the holiday season with love and kisses.

AN OFFICER AND A GENTLEMAN
by Rachel Lee

THE MAGIC OF CHRISTMAS
by Andrea Edwards

THE PENDRAGON VIRUS
by Cait London

Available December 1998
wherever Harlequin and Silhouette books are sold.

HARLEQUIN®
Makes any time special ™

Silhouette®

The Gifts of Christmas

Join three of your favorite historical romance authors as they celebrate the festive season in their own special style!

Mary Balogh
Merline Lovelace &
Suzanne Barclay

bring you a captivating collection of historical romances.

Indulge in the seasonal delights of Regency and medieval England and share in the discovery of unforgettable love with *The Gifts of Christmas.*

Available in November 1998, at your favorite retail store.

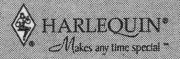

HARLEQUIN®

Makes any time special ™

Look us up on-line at: http://www.romance.net

PHGC872